Sitting down on the grass, she hugged her knees. Around her were the flat gray backs of the other houses, their facades broken up by the heavy, leafy fan shapes of the trees. She had a sensation of eyes watching her from the distant windows, wondering about her. . . .

Be very careful, she thought, *because if you make a mistake, you aren't going to escape! The enemy is watching, ready to pounce.*

She sat quite still, her heart thudding with the alarming realization of how easy it would be to make a slip, to remember wrongly—which was far worse than not remembering at all. The enemy was quick and alert, and the seeds of suspicion may already have been planted. . . .

Vonnie had come to St. John's Wood to bury the past—but by a twist of fate, the past might bury her!

THE NIGHT
MY ENEMY

ANNE MAYBURY

ACE BOOKS, INC.
1120 Avenue of the Americas
New York, N.Y. 10036

An *ACE STAR* BOOK, by arrangement with the Author.

Printed in the U.S.A.

I

It was just another of those thousands of cases where a girl met a man through a dog. But the result of their meeting was far removed from that of a simple love story.

As the great trans-Canada train drew in at Field, the little station in the heart of the Rockies, Vonnie left her compartment and stood waiting for the train to stop. Her eyes were lifted, fascinatedly, to the golden tops of the mountains and she had no way of knowing that the pattern of her easy, pleasant existence would change abruptly in a matter of minutes.

The colored conductor of Car No. 6—with its name, Mount Cascade, painted in gold letters on its door—stepped down onto the platform. He smiled at Vonnie and held out a hand to help her down.

She took the two deep steps and then, with a cry, hurtled over something that rushed past her.

Two people helped her to her feet. She stood shakily upright and laughed ruefully, first at a tall fair man and then at the conductor.

"You hurt, ma'am?"

She smiled into the broad, dark face, saying with wry amusement,

"No. And I hope the dog isn't!"

"Just look at him, ma'am!"

Vonnie looked. The dog was fine. He was beating it as fast as he could in the direction of the restaurant car. Vonnie watched him leap onto the train.

"Does he happen to be meeting a relative?" the fair man asked, laughing.

The conductor grinned.

"Why, him, suh? That's Smoky. He meets every train and the cook gives him a bone."

Vonnie rubbed one ankle against another.

"As the train stops here for ten minutes, he needn't have been in quite such a hurry! He didn't exactly look starved—"

"Starved. He's the best fed dog in Canada, ma'am! He's powerful big, too! In winter he pulls a sled for his master who has a small mine up there." The conductor nodded towards the mountains.

Another passenger called him and he left Vonnie standing with the tall, fair man.

They had seen each other many times during the journey from Montreal, had passed in the corridors, sat and read and had coffee in nearby seats in the observation car, eaten at adjoining tables in the restaurant. They had smiled vaguely, a little shyly. But it had taken a big brown dog hell-bent towards a beef bone to make them talk to one another.

The man was looking up at the mountains.

"It's a beautiful setting for a station!" His accent was English.

"Is this your first glimpse of the Rockies?"

"My very first!" He looked about him in quiet wonder.

The peaks were the color of gingerbread in the setting sun. Lodgepole pine, spruce and fir rose from the lower slopes of the mountains.

The man's head was lifted so that the sun glistened on his amber-colored hair. "I suppose there's a mass of wildlife up there watching us. Bear and elk and buffalo. Have you ever seen them?"

"I've seen bears at Jasper Park. The gardeners of the big hotels hate them because of the damage they do. But the showplaces would be dull without them. You know, in winter when the hotels are closed, they hibernate under the verandahs."

The man was watching her with interest.

"You know this part well?"

"No. My home is in Vancouver. I've stayed at Emerald Lake and Banff. But usually I'm only passing through on my way to stay with some friends on the eastern seaboard."

She glanced at him while she spoke—at the fine narrow head, the gray eyes that looked steadily and appraisingly at her, the mouth, kind and with a touch of humor, smiling friendlily. Then his eyes went past her. "Look!" he said.

She turned and saw the big brown dog sprawled on the platform with an outsize bone.

"And for that," Vonnie said, "I nearly broke my neck!"

Their immediate laughter broke the last vestige of shyness between them.

"You're English!" she said.

"I've been out here nine months working in Hamilton, Ontario."

They had turned together and were walking slowly towards the end of the platform where a road ran uphill to a cluster of frame houses with pointed roofs and little bright green lawns.

"Someone told me that I should see Vancouver and the Island while I'm here. So, as I had two weeks' break, before going back to England, I thought I'd spend it on the west coast."

"I hope you'll enjoy it," she said softly. "I think it's very beautiful."

"You've lived there all your life?"

"Almost. My people were English and they emigrated when I was very small. My father had a job at the university in Vancouver. He was a scientist."

"That's my profession," the man said with interest. "Only I'm on the industrial side. That's why I'm out here. I've been on loan to a chemical company in Hamilton. Then, after my holiday, I'm going up to have a look at northern British Columbia before I go home."

They stood together in the shadow of rich, dark spruce, looking up the short road.

"By the way," the Englishman said lightly, "in case we should meet again—and you never know—my name is Foster—Nigel Foster."

"I'm Yvonne Horne." She didn't add that everyone called her "Vonnie" because that sounded too friendly for passing traveling companions.

"And you live in Vancouver?"

"Just outside," she said, "on English Bay."

"And I suppose you ski and skate in the winter and play tennis and swim in the summer, just like all the other Canadian girls," he laughed.

"At weekends, yes."

The train conductor was making agitated signals. Nigel Foster saw them first.

"I think," he took her arm, "that if we don't sprint back, the train will go without us."

They ran and climbed on board, subsiding breathless in the observation car. The brown dog, sprawled with the bone between his paws, watched the train pull out and little knew what he had started.

In her small, compact compartment an hour later, Vonnie freshened up by putting on a dark green silk suit, did her face and combed her hair slowly, looking at herself in the mirror over the washbasin.

She had no vanity over her appearance. She had long

ago decided that sharing an apartment with Myra Ashlyn deflated any conceit one might have. For Myra was a radiant redhead and people always looked at her first—and looked a second time before they turned to Vonnie. Sometimes, when she was alone and looking in a mirror, she would think grudgingly, "You'll do!" Years of close companionship with Myra, of being absorbed in her vividness and warmth and vitality, had blinded her to her own attractiveness. Sometimes a man took Vonnie out and appraised her. "Your eyes are the color of sherry!" or, "Your eyebrows tilt when you laugh!" One man, with probably poetic leanings, told her that her hair was the color of wild mink.

She picked up her lipstick and drew it across the wide curved lines of her mouth. It was quite absurd to mind so much how she looked tonight because after this journey she would never see the Englishman again.

But he had asked her to dine with him and dinner on a train racing through the mountains could be a romantic affair. Nigel Foster had a drawing room and she was to go first of all and have a drink with him.

A date with a man on a train. She looked at her two small bottles of scent and chose her favorite—Rochas' *Femme*.

Then she opened a small chamois-leather folder which carried a few pieces of jewelry and chose a two-strand necklace of river pearls and a fire opal ring her father had given her on her birthday just before he died.

"Don't let anyone tell you opals are unlucky," he had said. "They're beautiful and in the olden days they were considered lucky. It was Sir Walter Scott who attributed the superstition of bad luck to the opal. The ancients loved it."

Vonnie loved it too. She stood in the swaying train and held up her hand, small, strong, square with well-kept nails. The opal glowed with green and crimson fire. She wove her way along the swaying train and found the door to Nigel Foster's drawing room compartment open. He said, laughing,

"This is a unique way of entertaining a lady for dinner, Miss Horne. But as you see, I do possess one armchair!"

Vonnie sat by the huge double window and accepted a sherry.

The train was now winding through the darkening evening, and between the railway and the craggy rising mountains ran the swift-moving, pounding Kicking Horse River.

Conversation was easy between them. The Englishman's present home was in London.

"I let my flat and stored my furniture when I came out here. So when I return, I've got to find myself another home!"

Vonnie said with longing,

"One of these days I'm going to give myself a long holiday and take myself off to see London. After all, I was born there—in Hampstead. It must be an exciting city."

"Most cities are exciting to strangers. The trouble with London for a Londoner is that it's too full of people and ears. But then," he added, "so is almost every other city."

"You've traveled a lot?"

He had, he said. Tokyo and Bombay and Cape Town. By the time they went in to dinner they had drifted into an easy companionship that was all the more wonderful because of the previous loneliness of the long journey across the continent.

There was salmon on the menu and Florida peaches and delicious cheese from the Oka monastery in Quebec. While they ate and talked, the train roared westward through the wide, silent mountain world.

Nigel's family home, he told her, was in Kent. His father had been a schoolmaster and was dead. A favorite aunt now lived with his mother in the old house facing the sea at Deal, where he had been born and had

10

lived so many years of his life. Something in their up-bringing, he said with a laugh, was parallel, wasn't it? The early years of both of them had been spent by the sea. Hers here, by this great unbroken expanse of Pacific Ocean; his within sight, on a clear day, of France. He told her about his childhood, about the ships that had become part of his boy's world, from small fishing boats to the white ship that ferried her way between Deal and Calais in summer.

Vonnie was fascinated. This was the England she wanted to see. She tried to visualize the two hundred and fifty year old house which had been his home with the time-blackened beams spanning the living room and the vast fireplace.

After dinner they sat in the observation car and had coffee while the train streaked through the mountains and the black night. And when they parted Nigel said,

"This has been the best-ever night in all my travels. Thank you for making it so."

Vonnie, who had made this journey across Canada several times, could have echoed his words. Instead, she just said, warmly, and with feeling,

"I've loved it, too. And thank you."

He saw her to her compartment.

"We meet in the morning! Good night." He smiled and left her.

That night, in bed, she turned restlessly and pulling aside the blind, peered out. Mountain and tree were faintly lit by a half moon but there was no sign of human life—no village, no hamlet, not even a shack to break the virgin stillness of that strange land. The wild animals had it to themselves. Out here, beneath the trees, they roamed or slept or perhaps watched the train go by with disinterested golden eyes.

Nigel had kept a place at the table for Vonnie when she went in to breakfast the following morning.

There was no time to linger. In a matter of minutes,

after a hasty meal, the train drew in at Vancouver Station.

Standing on the platform with her luggage Vonnie found Nigel by her side.

"I know you've got your home and your job here, but could you spare one evening to dine with me?"

Vonnie just managed to keep too much excitement out of her voice, saying with quiet pleasure, "I would love to, thank you."

"In which case"—he had an envelope and pencil ready —"I had better know your address, hadn't I?"

She gave it to him, watching him write it on the back of the envelope and thought with a faint dismay: he *could* lose it and he won't remember the address, so I may never see him again, after all!

"We met at the tail end of the journey, Miss Horne, but that's better than not meeting at all!"

Their hands touched. They smiled. "Good-bye," they said.

A redcap was collecting her luggage and Vonnie knew that Nigel was watching her as she followed the porter down the long platform.

She went with a strange new happiness through the barrier to the station hall.

And there, sweeping like a young goddess towards her, was Myra. In the moments it took them to meet, Vonnie registered the wild red-gold hair, the lovely violet-dark eyes, the voluptuous grace of the young figure in the vivid blue dress bearing down on her.

"Hello, honey!" Myra was completely uninhibited. She made no bones about liking people and showing them that she liked them.

Breaking from the hug Vonnie began, "I never expected—"

"To be met?" Myra swept a hand towards the luggage on the trolley. "But *I* expected *that!* You leave with two suitcases and return home with a brand new one *and* two hat boxes. For Pete's sake, what's that parcel?"

12

Vonnie laughed.

"A new type of bed I found for Gabriel."

Gabriel was the cat. Myra said protesting, "That was a waste of money! If he sleeps at all at night, it's on the tiles!"

"But he's growing old and I thought one day he'll probably like to have his own basket by the fire."

Myra said, "You think of everything, Vonnie! You always did!" Then to the redcap, "I've got a car outside. A red Pontiac. A.G. 400-32."

The porter nodded and began wheeling the dolly up the platform.

"Did you have a good journey?"

"Fine, except that, when we stopped at Field, I nearly broke my neck over a brown dog."

On first meeting Myra, people guessed her to be a model or an actress. Nobody believed that there was a good brain behind that lovely, flaming head and that she had bought a failing secretarial business and had built it up into a thriving agency.

Soon after she bought the little house on English Bay, Myra had dragged Vonnie to see it and suggested that as she disliked the idea of living alone, they might share the lower half. She planned to convert the top floor into a self-contained apartment and rent it.

At that time, Vonnie had only just started work in the publicity department of Meaker's Bay Stores. She had protested that she couldn't afford to share an expensive apartment, but that she would of course come and visit Myra just as often as she was asked. "And I *mean* often!" she had added firmly. "With a garden like that to sit in!"

Myra, pleading and cajoling, had, however, got her own way in the end.

"All I'm asking you for rent is sixty dollars a month, and that's only what you're paying now for that wretched one-room apartment. So there's no question of not being able to afford it!"

Sixty dollars was little enough by Canadian standards and Vonnie moved into the apartment on English Bay. She brought her own furniture to the large room looking over the garden and had had fun choosing one good picture, one lovely luster vase that would stamp the room with her own personality.

The arrangement worked perfectly. Their friendship, tried and tested through their college years, was never strained.

As the car turned the corner into the avenue of charming clapboard houses each in its own small plot of ground, Vonnie exclaimed, "You've bought some window boxes!"

"I decided that a yellow front door looked a bit out of place unless the color was carried somewhere else about the house. So, I had those window boxes painted. They look gay, don't they?"

They were filled with budding daffodils and with the wide open windows, the little house had a kind of singing gaiety. Vonnie felt, as she climbed out of the car, that she wouldn't be surprised to hear music. Then, halfway up the path, she stopped dead and listened. There *was* music.

"Oh heavens, I left the radio on," Myra laughed. "Well, at least you haven't arrived to the sound of a commercial!"

They carried the luggage into Vonnie's bedroom. The sun, breaking free of the clouds, broke over the room, and outside in the small, square garden, Gabriel—large and ponderous and tabby-colored—blinked at a fly.

Myra said airily that she had taken the morning off from work.

"What's the use of being your own boss if you can't use your hours as you want to?"

Vonnie unpacked a few things, lit a cigarette, and then stood and looked at her room. Going away was fun, but coming back was lovely. The room was furnished with beloved, familiar pieces she had kept from the sale

14

of her home after her father had died. They were antiques, brought out from England: a tallboy which everyone here called a "highboy"; a Regency desk with a mirror over it topped by a gilded cupid, and a little inlaid table on which Myra had set a pink luster bowl filled with irises.

Cream linen patterned with yellow springs covered the divan and the armchair; the curtains were of pale yellow silk and one gorgeous crimson silk cushion made a splash of color on the bed.

"Coffee's ready," Myra called, passing on her way to the living room.

Unlike Vonnie, Myra had kept nothing from her old home. The living room was furnished with modern pieces of Finland birch, uncluttered in design; cushions of jade and violet silk broke the pale, luminous quality of the wood.

They took their chairs onto the patio and curled up with sugar biscuits and cigarettes, drank their coffee and exchanged their news. Myra was like someone on the edge of subdued excitement. Her hands plucked at the folds of her dress and, at lulls in the conversation, her eyes flashed to Vonnie and away again as though part of her longed to tell her news and some other part held back. At last, she looked full at Vonnie and said with a rush of words, "I've had news of Brad."

Vonnie's eyes flew involuntarily to Myra's fingers as though expecting to see there the solitaire diamond she had worn for so short a time.

"And you're going to meet him again?"

"That's what I'm willing hard!" Her lovely face softened. "A year's parting is a pretty good test of whether you love someone or were merely infatuated for a time."

"Is Brad in Canada?"

Myra shook her red-gold head, picked up her cup, finished her coffee and said, "He's in New York, staying with the Harbornes. I had a letter yesterday from Linda Harborne; they're very old friends."

"You and Brad were right for each other," Vonnie said with emphasis. "If you could only meet again—"

"But I don't know how Brad feels. He might have got over caring for me. After all, our quarrel was pretty bitter—"

"And unnecessary!"

"Of course. Most quarrels are. But that doesn't make them any less final!" She lit a cigarette, blew a smoke ring and continued. "Linda rang me from New York and told me that he had asked about me. That's something. But if we're to meet again, it must come from Brad."

A great many men had wanted to marry Myra Ashlyn. Not one of them had meant anything to her except Brad Corcoran. They had met in New York and later, when he came to Vancouver to see her, they had become engaged. Vonnie never quite knew what the quarrel was about. Myra had said at the time that it had been a battle of wills, that if she didn't assert herself at the very beginning, Brad would dominate her life. And that was something she had no intention of letting anyone do! She was by nature strong and dominating herself, and her job—the charge and responsibility of a number of young girls—gave added strength to her personality. She should be loved and understood and that strong wayward flame in her controlled. Brad could have done that, Vonnie thought, watching Myra uncurl herself, get up, and go into the garden. She saw her walk, with that Junoesque poise of hers, towards the cat and pick him up, saw her rub her face against his heavy, protesting body and say, "No birds, Gabriel! You have some nice fish for lunch and leave the sparrows alone!"

Did Brad still love Myra? Or had a year made her vividness fade? Had the bitterness of what they had said on the night of the quarrel washed out all his desire for her?

Sitting there, watching Myra reach up to adjust a half coconut hanging from a branch of the cherry tree at the end of the garden, Vonnie remembered what it was like to be in love—and to get over it. Twice in her life she had nearly become engaged and looking back she knew that on neither occasion had it been more than a passing romance. She was three years younger than Myra and one day she, too, would fall in love. She would be guided by Myra's experience—if she really loved, she would see that nothing, no petty quarrel, no misunderstanding, no blind momentary stupidity jeopardized her happiness.

And at that moment, quite unbidden, there flashed across her mind a picture of the great brown dog on Field station, sprawled with the bone between his paws, watching the train pull out, his jaws open as though he were laughing at something—or someone. . . .

II

TWO DAYS LATER Nigel took Vonnie to dinner at a hotel that had a roof garden looking out over the Pacific.

She wore a new dress of blue silk organza threaded with silver; her slippers were dark blue straps with high silver heels.

Nigel said, appraising her across the table, "You're wearing my favorite color, Vonnie! I call it sapphire."

"So do I," she met his eyes and laughed, "though most men would call it 'blue' and leave it at that! I thought only artists knew the exact description of a color."

"I'm no artist," he assured her. "I'm a man of science. Though I'd change places tomorrow with Annigoni if I could."

They began to talk of art, the kind they both understood—not the abstract, but clear, self-explanatory work. Both of them admitted that they knew very little about painting or music, "but," they said in laughing unison, "I know what I like!"

The evening was perfect. They talked as though they had known one another for years, they danced between courses, drank a fine, sparkling white wine, and Nigel told her that he had seen the sauterne vineyards in France.

When it was time to leave he drove her, in the car he had hired for his stay, along the cliff road. They parked within sight of the sea and a small bay cluttered with yachts. To their right, trees grew thickly on the steep upward slope.

They sat quietly, conversation drifting to a few desultory remarks, deeply at peace together.

The stars trembled overhead; the wind was soft, coming all the way from Japan in the west. This was the moment, Vonnie thought, when a man put his arms around you and kissed you—not because he loved you but because romance was part of the lovely night.

Nigel Foster did not conform. He offered her a cigarette, lit it and his own, and then leaned back and stared at the reflection of the young moon, curved like a sickle on the water.

"If you've enjoyed this evening half as much as I have, will you come out with me again? And you *do* like music?"

She said happily, "Yes, thank you, to both those questions. I like music and I'd love to come."

Looking at him as she spoke, she knew that she was hoping, with the wild hope of dawning love, that he would want to go on and on seeing her. . . .

At the following weekend they went driving into the country and Vonnie showed him some of her favorite places. They wandered through woods, or found some tiny cove and lay in the sun.

On their last evening together, they went dancing again. Afterwards, they drove to the same lovely place between the woods and the sea.

She knew quite well, as he kissed her, that this was no romantic impulse.

"Vonnie—you once told me that you loved your life. But you don't love it too much to give it up, do you?"

His words, whispered against her hair, held a pleading and an urgency. But she had to hear him say what she knew he really meant. She stirred in his arms.

"It all depends—what I give it up for—"

"Love," he said, and turned her around and looked directly into her eyes. "I love you. But you know that, don't you?"

"We've known one another such a little while!" She held on frantically to the last defenses that protected her heart. Something deep inside her, even now, was afraid of this moment, as though it were only romance, or infatuation, or an impulse on a lovely night. . . .

"It's real, Vonnie," he said.

And then suddenly she knew that it *was* reality for him, as for herself. She turned and lifted her face, and said in a shaken voice: "I love you, Nigel. I've loved you —all the time—"

A long time later, he said, "Tomorrow I leave for Yellowknife. But it's only a temporary parting." He laughed softly, "Do you think you'll like living in England, my little Canadian?"

"Or Katmandu or Timbuktu!" she cried recklessly. "It doesn't in the least matter. We'll pitch a tent in the Sahara if you like."

Time stopped meaning very much. But presently the moon rose over the bay and Nigel stirred, giving her a gentle push.

"You're a witch, Vonnie! And if I don't take you home now, I won't leave for Yellowknife in the morning!"

Vonnie was glad that Myra's bedroom was in darkness when she let herself into the apartment. Just for tonight she wanted to hold her memory of the evening to herself. Gabriel, on the prowl, rubbed himself against her legs. She picked him up and set him in his new basket in the kitchen and then crept to her room.

She undressed and lay in the darkness, trying to look into her suddenly new and radiant future. Such little things changed the pattern of life! Just a great brown dog bounding for a bone . . .

Vonnie woke to a brilliant morning. She remembered her mother saying how short spring seemed in Canada. Scarcely had the snow melted and the trees burst into bud than summer was there, blazing across the land! Unlike England, her mother had said wistfully, where spring is long and sweet and lingering.

She padded in bare feet to the window and thought with longing how good it would be to be festive on such a morning. To put on a gay dress—the new green and white striped cotton with the swinging skirt, the enormous white-flower earrings, her green sandals. Standing in front of the mirror, Vonnie could imagine the lifted eyebrows and the grins if she arrived at the office looking dressed for the beach. Mike Garham, from the art department, would perch himself on her desk and grin at her and say, "What about a date tonight, sweetie?"

But then Mike had been suggesting that date for the past six months and still couldn't take "No" for an answer. Not that Mike mattered. Refusals whetted his appetite. If she had gone out with him when he first asked her he would have been looking at her now with a disinterested eye. She was glad she had no entanglements to get out of, glad her love for Nigel was deep and uncomplicated. . . . She reached for a light navy linen dress, regretted that she must wear such a sober color on such a lovely day, and slid into it. She brushed her hair back, sleeking it down, drew coral lipstick across the wide, deep curves of her mouth, and went into the kitchen.

Myra, who as her own mistress cared nothing for office sobriety, wore a dress of yellow Indian cotton. With her red-gold hair and her lovely skin, she looked like some exotic, animated flower as she came, rustling in stiffened petticoat, into the kitchen.

Vonnie made toast. Myra crossed to the percolator and took it to a cream laminated-top table in the dining alcove by the open window.

"Where did you eat last night?"

"Manetti's."

"For a man who's a stranger here, Nigel certainly knows where to take a girl!" Myra observed. "Do you want your coffee poured out yet?"

"Please." Vonnie carried the toast rack to the table.

"And you had a good time?"

"Lovely!"

Myra shot her a quick, quizzical glance and went to the front door to retrieve the two morning papers. Vonnie poured coffee and sat with the cup in her two hands.

She said, as Myra sat down and reached for the toast, "Nigel wants me to go to England."

Myra's violet eyes opened and narrowed.

"Just like that? Come to England and I'll show you the sights? Well, that's fine. But—"

"He wants me to go for good. Myra—I—we're in love."

"I've known for the past week that *you* were!" Myra said matter-of-factly. "But I wasn't so sure about Nigel. The few times I've seen him, he seems too reserved to show feelings—but that's an Englishman all over! You do mean that you're going to be married—or is this one of those unconventional love affairs?"

Vonnie sipped her coffee.

"We shall be married."

"He *asked* you?"

Vonnie said quietly, "That was understood—"

"But he didn't produce an engagement ring."

Vonnie put down her cup.

"Last night we—knew we loved one another. We didn't think of anything else—we just knew that the future was ours. Nigel had to leave today for Yellowknife. When he comes back—"

Myra bit into buttered toast.

"Is he coming back here before he leaves for England?"

"If he can. Yes."

"And if he can't? What happens?"

"What—happens? Well—I suppose I shall go to England. Why?"

"What I mean," Myra said steadily, "is that you've known Nigel for a fortnight and that fortnight is his holiday. To him, a stranger, I suppose Vancouver has a glamor. A little romance is part of that holiday. Is it just that, or—?"

Vonnie slammed down her cup and spilled coffee in her saucer.

"Or is it real and lasting?"

"That's what I'm asking."

"In other words, you're inferring that all Nigel wanted was a passing romance."

"I'm just asking if this is a passing love affair or if it is forever. I like Nigel and I don't believe he'd say he was in love with a girl unless he really was. But—look, honey, I'm older than you and I've had knocks. It's just that— well, that I don't want you to be hurt."

"I won't be hurt," Vonnie said quietly. "It's forever."

"Then that's wonderful." But the small frown remained between Myra's eyes. She made a resolute effort and smiled.

"Take no notice of me! I've had the sort of experiences that make me skeptical until a ring is on a girl's finger, and even then—" but her face was clouded and Vonnie knew she was remembering Brad.

Before and after that unhappy affair, Myra, with her beauty and her vividness had run the gamut of all invitations from a weekend on a yacht sailing between the islands to a semi-permanent setup in a luxury flat as mistress of a timber merchant. And she had smiled sweetly and said, "Odd as it may seem from my looks, I'll only live with a man who's my husband!"

"If it's an official engagement, I'd better drop Nigel a note of congratulations," she was saying.

"It won't be in the social columns of the papers, if that's what you mean. Nor will I be having a big engagement party. Not here, at any rate."

"I hope you meet again before he leaves for England."

"Oh, he'll manage it somehow," Vonnie said easily. "If he can't get here for a couple of days, I'll go to Montreal for a day or two before he sails."

"I think," Myra said quite definitely, "that a friendly note from his girl's best friend might warm his heart. If you give me his address—"

"I can't. He didn't give me one."

Myra didn't look up. Her hand reached out for the sugar bowl.

"He's going to write to me when he gets to Yellowknife," Vonnie said quickly. "He's motoring up with some man from Toronto. I'll have his address soon."

"Yes. Yes, of course—" Myra said vaguely, meaninglessly.

A silence fell between them and neither could break it.

At every post that week, Vonnie looked for a letter. And each day she would tell herself, "I shall hear tomorrow."

Two weeks passed, however, and Vonnie was forced to remember Myra's doubtful enthusiasm.

She never once asked if a letter had arrived. But Vonnie knew that she had never let go of her suspicion that for Nigel this was just a holiday romance.

Vonnie seized upon every reason for his silence. There had been an accident, or he was ill.

In either case, someone would contact her. She tried to recall the firm for which he had said he worked in England. Not that that would help because she could not send an inquiry there. You didn't chase a man to his office half across the world! The only thing she could do which was not too blatant was to ring up his Vancouver hotel and ask if they had been given a forwarding address. She learned that they had not. Then she put through a call to the hotel at which she knew he had stayed in Montreal. There, too, they could tell her nothing of his movements. As far as they knew, they said briefly and politely, he had no intention of returning.

On Saturday morning at the end of the second week, the postman was late.

They had taken their second cups of coffee out onto the tiny patio when they heard him tramping up the front path.

Vonnie flew to the door. There were three letters in

the postbox. Two for Myra and a post order catalog from a Montreal store for her.

With the now familiar heavy heart, she carried them into the garden. Myra looked at the envelope Vonnie held.

"And a mail order catalog for you. Now that you had such a spending spree in Montreal, you're going to get these on every possible occasion and you'll be asked to buy everything from a Paris hat to a washing machine!" She was talking to bridge the gap of this moment of disappointment she knew Vonnie had felt. Her fingers were lazily slitting open her largest envelope.

"And all that goes for me, too!" She held up a fur store catalog. On the cover was a girl swathed in white furs. "My dream for myself!" she laughed. "Arctic fox and diamond earrings and a Cadillac to take me home! And all I've got is a Pontiac and rhinestones for my ears! Oh dreams!" She was opening the other letter, saying, "Airmail from England? I don't know who—" She had unfolded the sheet of notepaper. Her eyes flashed across the lines and she sat bolt upright in her chair.

"Just listen to this. Vonnie—"

"Go ahead!" Vonnie pulled herself out of her cloud of beaten hope.

"Did you know I had an uncle in England?"

"You've mentioned him from time to time."

"He was quite a well-known artist in his day. He's old —actually he's my father's uncle," her face had a sudden tight, hard look. "After forgetting our existence from the moment we left England when I was five, here's a letter from him!"

"He has probably only just found out where you live."

"He knew perfectly well that Father emigrated to Canada and settled in Vancouver. But he was too busy becoming a successful portrait painter to bother about us. He never wrote to us or even sent a Christmas card!" When Myra was angry her violet eyes would deepen and her face would go white. It was white now. "When my father died, he didn't even write to my mother! And now, just because *he's* ill, and probably got a conscience —odd how people develop them when they think they're dying!—he writes to me!"

"Well, it won't do any harm to reply."

"It isn't just a reply he wants," Myra retorted. "It's an invitation to England for four weeks, all expenses paid."

"But that's wonderful!"

"Wonderful to see England, yes. But not to see *him!* I'm not going over there to play the loving niece ready to drop everything to keep him company in his old age. Why should I? He never bothered to find out if my mother was provided for when my father died. And he could have afforded to. He's a bachelor and he has made a lot of money out of painting fashionable portraits."

"And now he's ill and old and lonely—"

"He's apparently ill, but I don't know the rest. After all, how do I know anything about his domestic circumstances? He may have some devoted housekeeper. He's certainly got Fenella, my cousin who lives in London— though she doesn't write to me either." A faint impish grin touched Myra's face. "I don't wonder at that! I have a dim memory that when we were very little girls and used to meet, we hated the sight of one another. I don't know what she does or even if she still lives in London. But I'm perfectly certain, from what Father told us on the few occasions he talked about Uncle Joss, that he has always been first of all concerned with his own well-being."

"But you'll go to England?"

Myra relaxed slightly.

"I'll go," she said. "Oh yes, I'll go! And I'll see to it that I have the time of my life." She tossed the letter onto the table, then leaned over, reading from it. "He puts it this way: 'You'd better come as soon as you can. Old men with hearts like mine count their lives in days, not months.' He also says that if I have to leave my job in order to go, he'll see that I don't lack funds till I find other work on my return. Well, he doesn't have to worry on that score! I can leave Belle in charge of the business; she likes responsibility anyway."

"You'll be going at once?"

"I suppose so," she pushed back her red-gold hair with both hands. "I wish you could come, too."

"I wish I could."

"But you *could!*" Myra said, eyes bright with impulse. "Vonnie, listen. Suppose you let me get your air ticket for you and we find you a hotel near this house in St. John's Wood where Uncle Joss lives. We could probably meet quite often. It would be such fun, for me!"

"But not for me!" Vonnie said lightly. "I'd have the fearful thought of having to return to no job! Besides, I couldn't let you pay my fare. It's a lovely thought, Myra, but you're not Mr. Onassis or Mr. Gulbenkian—"

"I'm suggesting it for *my* sake! It'd be my indulgence, Vonnie, because *I'd* enjoy it so if you were there. And if that boss of yours wouldn't give you a month's leave, then you'd find something when you got back. I wish you did shorthand and typing, then I'd find you a really good job."

"But I just know how to do layouts for store catalogs and the names of the various printing types and the difference between half-tone and line blocks." Vonnie lay back and closed her eyes. "I'd give a lot to go to England. But not like that, with the thought at the back of my mind that I'd be coming back to no job in an overcompetitive market!" Then she opened her eyes and looked at Myra. "When will you go?"

"In a week or two. There's nothing to keep me here."

Nothing, Vonnie thought, to keep either of them here! For Myra, the fact that Brad Corcoran had come to New York had roused a lovely hope that had died as the days went by without contact from him. By now, he must have returned to San Francisco where he lived, with neither effort nor desire to see her.

She thought with a shudder: We've both been living

on hope these past few weeks; and we've both seen it die. . . .

But why? What made a man say "I love you. I want to be with you always!" and then go out of your life without a word? Impulse? A brief infatuation? An inability to resist a romantic situation? Or, perhaps, a little of all three?

Well, it happened! You fell for the whole lovely story, dared to dream; and then when the dream was in tatters, you cast the shreds away and picked up your life again and went on with it. The secret was never to look back. To remember that life is not the past nor the future but the everlasting 'Now.'

Myra stretched her full, supple body and said, "Thank heaven it's Saturday and I have a weekend to mull it over!"

"Thank heaven it's Saturday, and *I* can do some gardening!" Vonnie tossed back and crossed to a bed of wallflowers and began weeding it. Once, when she turned her head, she saw that Myra had gone into the house and was at her bureau. She thought wryly that that was where she was so wise. She was warm and good, but she was on the beam every time. She didn't waste her life in indecision. Vonnie knew perfectly well, as she saw a pen fly across notepaper, that Myra was writing her acceptance of her Uncle Joss's invitation by return of post.

The next few days were a flurry of excitement. Myra wasn't going to arrive in London like a relation from the backwoods, she said. Since her fare was being paid for her, she was going to splash in glamor. But she wouldn't let Vonnie go shopping with her.

She said, "I'm not going to rub it in that I've got this chance and am leaving you behind."

Vonnie insisted on seeing everything when Myra, who could walk into any clothes and carry them out of the shop without need of alterations, arrived home after her shopping sprees. The two beautiful silk suits, the coat with the enormous collar that made her look like an actress sweeping into some scene of high drama on the stage, the silk jersey dresses.

"I'm even going to buy a couple of hats," Myra said.

Hats to cover that glorious red head! It was sacrilege and Vonnie said so.

Myra laughed.

"But you see, I intend to find someone to take me to dinner at the Savoy and lunch at Claridges; I shall go to a reception at Canada House and wangle an invitation (if I'm allowed to stay that long!) to see Wimbledon tennis. You want hats at those places. And shoes. I think I'll buy those crocodile ones I saw in Marsh's."

III

On Monday, only a week before Myra was to leave, Vonnie came home from the office to find, to her surprise, that she was already home.

She dropped her handbag and light coat onto a chair, commenting lightly, "You're early! Have your staff struck?"

Myra stood very straight and still.

"I'm going to see Brad." She could not contain the news.

The quiet level tone belied the vivid, living beauty of her face.

"You mean, he's coming to Vancouver?"

Myra remained very taut and tall. It was as if she dare not trust herself to move in case she walked out of some magic circle into a reality where there would be no Brad.

"Linda has written from New York asking if I'll join her family for a holiday in Mexico. They've been offered a villa at Cuernavaca for a few weeks. Six of them are going and Brad is to be in the party. We're to leave New York in ten days' time—"

"But—" Vonnie began.

Myra cut her short: "And he knows I'm going to be asked! Linda underlined that bit. She says that it was only then that Brad said definitely he would join the party."

"But you *can't* go! You're going to England."

Myra put up her hands and made the characteristic gesture of pushing back her thick bright hair. Not a shadow of doubt crossed her face.

"Oh, I shall write to Uncle Joss and say I've been held up. That I'll go to England later."

"There may be no other opportunity. People with serious heart conditions don't always recover—"

"Then I'll be terribly sorry. But nothing—*nothing* is going to stop me from going to Mexico!" She looked at Vonnie. "You think I'm being hard, don't you? Well, perhaps I am. But Uncle was hard all those years to my father and mother—"

Vonnie got up and went to the window. Rain was falling from the west like tiny, bright arrows shooting at the windows. She watched it in silence.

"All right," came Myra's defiant voice from behind her, "so I'm being selfish and hard! But it's my happiness, Vonnie! Second chances don't often come to us and when they do we have to take them or be sorry for the rest of our lives."

Vonnie turned and caught the lovely pleading gaze.

"This isn't just a holiday spree," Myra continued. "*You* know that! This is my life—my whole reason for living! I want to marry Brad, I love him and I'll never stop loving him. I want to make a home with him, have his children—isn't that important, too?"

"Perhaps if you explained why you couldn't go," Vonnie said gently, "he might love you the more for it."

"Or he might think that compassion for an old relative wasn't the honest reason. He might think I was going because—well, because Fenella, my cousin, and I are Uncle Joss's only living relatives and I was cashing in."

"If he loves you, Brad wouldn't think that. When you come back from England—"

"But I'm not *going* to England!"

"Even if you did," Vonnie insisted, "Brad will contact you if he still loves you."

"Oh Vonnie, don't put men, even the man you love, on a pedestal!" Myra cried. "Heaven knows why some girl hasn't snapped Brad up during these past six months!

31

Because a man doesn't remain loyal and loving to a memory for long—not these days. My suspicion is that they never did; it's just a myth they themselves created to shame women into doing the same!"

Vonnie said, half-puzzled, half-understanding, "What are you really trying to say?"

"That it's a wonderful thing that Brad has stayed unmarried and still wants to see me. But he's a man and human and he won't carry a torch for me much longer. Maybe there's a girl down in Mexico, and if I don't go, *she'll* be there one moonlit night to sweep him off his feet. You think I'm going to let that happen just because an old man I haven't seen for seventeen years, and who has never even written to me for Christmas, suddenly decides to summon me?" She turned and swept across the room, her skirt swishing. She looked arrogant and angry. Then she sat down at her bureau and took out a piece of notepaper and laid it on the blotting pad.

"This," she said and picked up her pen, "is my answer to everyone. Linda and Uncle Joss—and *you!*" She laughed, scrawled a few lines and then read what she had written aloud.

Dear Linda,
I'll be on that plane come hell and high water! Meet you on May 23rd. And I'll tell you then just how wonderful I think your invitation is. At the moment I can't write any more because I'm nearly berserk with happiness.
Tell Brad—or no, don't tell him anything except that I'm coming.

Bless you a million.
Myra.

She laid the sheet of paper down on her bureau and looked at Vonnie.

"And there we have it! Oh, Vonnie, go and mix us a drink and don't look as though I'd sold my soul! If someone you loved—someone you had once promised to marry and then broken with because of some idiotic row —came back into your life, what would *you* do?"

Vonnie said, quietly and honestly, "Just what you're doing!" and went out to the kitchen to fetch ice for the drinks.

By the time they had had supper and cleared away, it was raining hard.

Myra said, "Perhaps there's something worth looking at on television."

"Probably, but I think you should first of all write to your uncle. It's just as well, if you're postponing your visit, to let him know as soon as possible."

Myra dropped her hand from the television set, swung herself into a chair and said, "I suppose you're right. But it's not the sort of letter I'll like writing." She hunched her shoulders. "In fact, it's going to make me feel bad, even though I don't believe I should have a conscience over it. Oh, Vonnie, just look at that rain!"

"It saves us watering the garden. Don't worry!" She wandered around the room.

"Looking for something?"

"Yes. My book. The one I especially got out of the library for you to read. The one on London—"

"Don't rub it in!"

"I'm sorry," she laughed. "I wasn't trying to. But I thought, as you won't be needing it now, I'll return it and get the new Elwin novel out tomorrow for myself."

Myra didn't seem to hear her. She had her hands held out in front of her and was studying the pink, well-kept nails.

"After all," she said slowly, "it isn't as though Uncle were fond of me."

"You've said your say, honey!" Vonnie laughed. "You don't have to go on justifying to me!"

"—or as though he knew me very well," Myra went on. "Why, he doesn't even know what I look like—he wouldn't recognize me from the girl next door!" She lifted her eyes and gave Vonnie a long, thoughtful stare.

The clock struck the half hour after eight. Neither of them heard it. Their eyes were focused on each other, and across Myra's face there flashed a sudden vivid excitement.

"Uncle Joss doesn't—even—know—what—I—look—like! Do you realize what that means?"

"Of course. Every word of it. He doesn't even know what you look like. And you're not going to England yet. Now forget it! You're not the type to have things on your conscience, so there's nothing more to say."

"Isn't there?" Myra's eyes were bright.

"Knowing you, I really don't see why, having made up your mind, you're harping on it!"

"If there were telepathy between us, I wouldn't have to explain. As it is—well, Vonnie, you see—"

"Look," Vonnie broke in matter-of-factly, "suppose you put on a coat and let's go for a walk and let the rain wash your guilt complex away?"

"But I haven't *got* one!" Myra was impatient. "I'm trying to say something important to you and you won't catch on! Vonnie, listen! Uncle Joss hasn't seen me since I was a little girl." She got up and walked in a circle around the room, still talking. "So anyone could go to England and pretend to be me and Uncle Joss would never know. Just for four weeks, anyone could stay at Uncle Joss's house and play at being Myra Ashlyn. *You*, Vonnie—"

"Me? You must be quite crazy!"

"But I'm not! It came to me like a kind of inspiration. The answer to the whole problem—the obvious answer, Vonnie. You could go to England in my place and no one would be the wiser."

"Except you and me—and our consciences! And the passport officers and—"

"But you'd travel to England on your own passport. Then when you got there you'd take on my identity;

you'd seal the passport away in an envelope, hide it in your suitcase and no one would ever find out."

"I suppose it hasn't occurred to you that my handwriting is so unlike yours that it would give me away at once. You wrote to Uncle Joss, remember, only a week ago!"

"Well, work hard at copying my handwriting and my signature. You should know what it looks like by now. And anyway, why should you have to write anything that they'll see while you're over there? If worse comes to worse, you've hurt your hand, sprained a thumb, done anything you like—and writing with a bandage on is a most difficult thing to do."

"You think of everything!" Vonnie said dryly.

"Yes, I do, don't I?" Myra cried with what seemed an innocent delight. "And it would be the perfect answer!"

"Except that it's too crazy to contemplate."

"But it isn't! Look at the facts." Myra stood in front of Vonnie, leaning a little towards her so that the subtle scent of Guerlain's *Jicky* made a sea of sweetness around her. "*I* shan't go in any case. That means Uncle Joss will be disappointed. You know how little I feel about him after the way he has ignored my family! But, don't you see, after that wretched business with Nigel, going to England would be just the thing to take you right out of yourself. You'd get away, see fresh sights, fresh people. Vonnie, *think*—"

"I am! And the more I do, the more incredible the whole idea seems."

"Uncle Joss said in his letter that he'd see that I had enough money to tide me over on my return if I had to give up my job. Well, so that needn't worry you. And working for Marsh's isn't the peak of your career, you've always told me that! Just think, Vonnie, of all the arguments for going! And against that, what is there? Just that you're taking my place. Well, there's no harm in that. You're not impersonating me without my consent, and I'm sure you aren't breaking a law. You'd just be doing a great kindness. If Uncle Joss is so ill that he might die at any moment, think of the happiness you'd be giving him. He'll never know that you've taken my place, and to him it would be an ignorance that was bliss. Because he'd love you, Vonnie, he wouldn't be able to help it! And so he'd be really happy."

Vonnie shot up from her chair, crossed the room, and flung the window open wide.

She felt that Myra was watching her, that she was trying, passionately, to force her will upon her.

"You're stifling me!" Vonnie cried.

"That's your unnecessary conscience going to work!" Myra said softly. "Just tell it to lie down! Don't you see that every single one of the people involved would be happier if you decided to go to London in my place? Uncle Joss for one—what does it matter whether you're really his niece or not? Just anyone could be a relative for all that he has ever bothered to find out about me! You'd enjoy it, also, because you want to see England and it would be particularly good for you to get away at this time. And I—well, for me it would be the perfect solution! Just think, Vonnie. Who'd suffer?" Her voice was soft, gentle and cajoling. She waited. "Well? *Who?*"

If I were honest, Vonnie thought, I'd have to answer that no one would suffer. It was so feasible that it was almost frighteningly easy. Just four weeks of being someone else and then back again, with no harm done and everyone's wishes granted.

"No," she said loudly and turned around and faced Myra. "No, of course I won't go to England!"

"All right, honey! Then that's that!" Myra turned, unperturbed, and put a dance record on the gramophone and hummed the tune. She began to dance slowly, dreamily, with a little smile on her face as though it didn't matter, anyway. Or, Vonnie thought watching her, as though she knew she would get her own way in the end? But of course she wouldn't. . . .

That night, however, the outrageous suggestion came between Vonnie and sleep. If she went—*if* she went—then who would be the wiser? And perhaps, when she returned, Vancouver would be no longer haunted by her own happy ghost walking with Nigel by the sea, sailing with him around the myriad little wooded islands, driving with him along the lovely coast road. . . . There was so much to recommend it and only two things against. One, that it was deception. But it was not criminal, and it was anything but cruel! On the contrary, it was deception in a good cause, for the happiness of three people. The other argument against it was doubt as to her own ability to carry it through. To live and talk as though she were Myra. But there again, the argument was weak. For no one at the house in London had seen Myra since she was a little girl of five. No one knew how she spoke, what her idiosyncrasies were, even what she looked like. Hair changed color these days with a mere rinse; features were not sufficiently formed to be recognizable seventeen years later. And anyway, if Uncle Joss Ashlyn had not written to Myra all these years, what did he know about her? There was not even a photograph for comparison between the real and the impersonation.

On Monday Vonnie walked part of the way home from the office through the park. Something about its green lushness in the sunlight brought the pain of Nigel's silence clamping down on her like a vice. Beauty hurt! Beauty brought memories, in loneliness, of old past happiness . . . she had clung to the belief that as the days passed, the hurt would fade until soon she would be able to think of him and of that lovely fortnight as an episode too good to be true, an ideal you touched and lost again because it was too beautiful (for one person at least) for permanence.

But this common sense outlook wasn't working! At unexpected moments the pain came back, fierce as ever, and with it the questions that would now never be answered. Was it just a romantic holiday interlude for him? Had he, perhaps, been serious at the time but, leaving Vancouver, had he changed his mind? Or maybe there was some other girl in England and he lacked the courage to break with her. Or a wife . . . So many possibilities—and nothing to ease the pain of questioning. . . .

Nothing?

And then she remembered Myra's incredible idea. A journey abroad, new sights and sounds, new experiences —even the effort of trying to be someone else for a month would so absorb her that perhaps she would find memory of Nigel pushed from her mind. A respite. And when she returned to Canada surely the memory would have become dimmed by it.

Vonnie was setting long, cool drinks on the small wrought iron table on the porch when Myra returned home.

She came straight through the house and stood watching Vonnie, saying, "You know what we did this morning?"

"What?"

"We forgot to arrange who'd get the food in for tonight! You didn't . . . ?"

"I didn't give it a thought! I walked home through the park and I—was thinking about things and—"

"Never mind, we've probably got something in the ice box."

"A few chicken bones and a lettuce," Vonnie laughed. "I'll go out and get something."

"Oh, don't bother," Myra flung herself into a chair. "We've got tins and some cheese. There's enough for a feast if we only look! What's in that jug?"

"A little gin, a lot of orange and loads of ice."

"Wow!" said Myra softly and poured herself out a glass.

Vonnie watched her light a cigarette. She said, tentatively, "Have you written and told your Uncle Joss you're not going to England?"

"Not yet."

"You should have! But—"

The violet eyes lifted in amusement, dark gold brows tilted. There was mischief in Myra's face.

"But what, Vonnie?" she asked softly.

She's a witch, Vonnie thought without resentment. She has known all along that I'll go! She took a breath, paused and then spoke the fatal words.

"You don't need to write. It's quite wrong and I'm not a bit certain it isn't criminal. I mean, even if the person whose name is taken condones it, it might still be a criminal act?"

Myra chuckled as though the law was a joke. "I'm quite sure there's nothing really criminal in an impersonation known and accepted by the two people most concerned. Who would care, anyway? Certainly not the police. Only Uncle Joss and he'll never find out. Vonnie —you've made up your mind to go, haven't you?"

Myra sat in a chair, leaning forward, her elbows on her knees, her hands around her glass. Over its rim her eyes danced and approved; her left foot in her high-heeled bronze slipper made little tapping movements as though she wanted to get up and dance.

"Yes," Vonnie said steadily. "It's crazy, and heaven knows how I'll manage it, but I'll go to London!"

"And that's the most sensible decision I've ever heard you make!"

"I wonder!" Vonnie said cautiously.

"Of course it is, because nothing will go wrong. Nothing *can* go wrong!" Myra told her with superb confidence.

Vonnie gave a week's notice at the office the following day, and to her amazement her chief suggested that if she postponed going until the end of the month, he would give her a month's leave. She was touched and grateful, but explained that a relative was ill and delay was impossible.

He said, "Very well. I'm sorry to lose you, Miss Horne. When you return, look me up. I'm sure we can find a place for you."

It was tantamount to saying that, although they had no intention of keeping her as a salary-earning employee on their books, they did not want to lose her altogether.

Her job, then, was more or less safe.

There were papers to be put in order, clothes to buy, Myra's plane tickets (one from Vancouver to Montreal, one from there to England) to be taken over.

"Suppose," Vonnie said in alarm, "your Uncle Joss sends someone to meet me at the airport?"

"Well, what if he does?"

"And he sees my passport?"

"You'll be through all that fussation before you get to the barrier, so you'll have plenty of time to put your papers away. Don't worry. Anyway," she continued, "I've only had this one brief note saying he's looking forward to seeing me and to let him know the date of my arrival."

"Then I think we'll be vague about it. We'll say the—" Vonnie considered, "the 20th of May."

"But the plane ticket from Malton will get you there on the 18th."

"That's fine. It'll give me two days to get my breath and gather my courage."

Myra said, with her particular brand of airy confidence, "Honey, you won't need much courage for this! Just tell yourself you're Myra Ashlyn. Little Myra who used to visit that big old Victorian house in St. John's Wood and slip into the studio when Uncle Joss wasn't looking and jab her finger into the wet paint!" she laughed. "I did, you know! Until Mother caught me with bright sticky colors all over my fingers. I was given a jolly good talking-to for that! I remember because Mother said Uncle Joss would never again send me a nice present on my birthday if I went into the studio without being asked. Well, I didn't go into the room again—I wanted nice presents on my birthday and at Christmas. And a lot of good it did me! We left for Canada soon after and I never had another present or even a card! Nice man, Uncle Joss!"

"You make me wonder whether I'm going to meet an ogre!"

"Oh no," Myra said sensibly. "Just a rather selfish old bachelor. But you'll cope. You'll charm him, Vonnie. His type likes gentle people far more than some opinionated flamboyant type like me! You'll be just the niece he dreams about!"

"Flattery," Vonnie said dryly, "will get us nowhere. Now what about my trying to copy your awful signature—just in case I have to use it?"

In the hectic days before she left, the ethics of what she was about to do were lost under the growing doubt as to whether she would be able to cope. Or would something, some small unexpected thing, give her away?

What could? She would seal up her personal papers. To her friends in Vancouver, she explained that she was leaving for England and would let them know her address. Only one thing presented a difficulty and that was the fact that travelers' checks must be in her own name. But then she would make certain no one came to the bank with her when she cashed them. She was Vonnie Horne until the moment she walked through the barrier at London Airport. From then on, she must forget her own identity, forget that she worked in the P.R.O. Department of Marsh's Stores. Suddenly something struck her.

"Myra, I can't type!"

"Well, what about it?"

"Uncle Joss knows you've got your own secretarial agency because you told him in that first letter. Suppose he wants some typing done?"

"Then you've hurt your right hand."

"I won't remember that all the time!"

"You can have an impacted bone or whatever it's called. You slipped somehow or other getting on or off the plane. You're told to rest the finger. So you don't type. I know—" Myra rose, went to her room and came back with a ring. "See if that'll fit one of your fingers."

It was a large oval topaz set in gold and one of Myra's favorites.

"I can't take that with me!"

"Don't be silly. Put it on."

It fitted Vonnie's middle finger.

"Wear it all the time. It's big enough to make you remember that that finger has got to be out of use so far as pressure or typing is concerned. That'll take care of that!"

"Suppose I lost it—"

"It's insured and if you wear it all the time, as you'll have to to remind you, you won't lose it, will you?" Myra said practically. "And by the way, that blue silk suit I bought, the one with the low-cut collar, is quite wrong on me. That wretched persuasive assistant made me buy it. It's much too tight in places where I'm most sensitive to my weight. Try it on for size."

"It's a lovely suit. I'll buy it from you if it fits."

"Oh, for land's sake!" Myra whipped out of the room and came back with the suit over her arm. "Blue isn't my color either. But it's yours."

It was dark sky blue and it had a wide, deep collar and three-quarter sleeves.

Vonnie slid out of the dark green cotton dress.

"What a little thing you are!" Myra said grudgingly. "The sort men love to cherish!"

"I hadn't noticed it!" Vonnie's tone was without bitterness. She got into the suit and smoothed it over her hips.

"It's lovely on you," Myra stood back, appraisingly. "The skirt wants shortening and the sleeves too. But that's easy."

"I just can't accept an expensive suit," Vonnie began to protest.

"Take what the gods give you and enjoy it. I owe you more than an off-the-rack suit for what you're doing."

"You might remember that I'm doing this partly for myself, too, and for your Uncle Joss—"

"Look, honey, you'd better stop calling him 'Your Uncle Joss.' You've got to look on him as *your* relative from now on. So you'd better start that way. Uncle Joss, and Fenella Ashlyn, your cousin. I think that's all you have to bother about. Anyway, apart from those, you know as much about my family as I know myself!"

IV

VONNIE LEFT for England some days before Myra flew
to New York on the first lap of her holiday in Mexico.
The people in the upstairs apartment had promised to
keep an eye on the place for them and to look after
Gabriel. In return Myra offered them the use of the garden while she was away. Vonnie's letters must not be
sent on, but she made certain that there would be nothing of importance that could not wait until she returned.

She answered every letter, paid bills, put her affairs
in order, "as though" she told herself, "I were never
coming back!"

A thought kept crossing her mind that there was still
a chance that Nigel might write to her. But it was a pale
and very remote chance. She must be strong and face
the fact that he was in the past and the past was gone
forever. Now, there was the future and she must give all
her energy to believing in herself and her success. There
was nothing dangerous in what she was about to do, and
yet it needed courage. It was a test for her wits and
awareness. And she wouldn't, she mustn't, fail. . . .

Myra saw her off at the airport. In her note case Vonnie had her address in Mexico in case of an emergency.
She was traveling with three suitcases—one a splendid
new one Myra had bought and which had her initials
on it. All of them were lightly tied with labels bearing
Vonnie's own name. Somehow, between leaving the
plane at London Airport and reaching the barrier, she
must manage to remove them, just in case Joss Ashlyn
sent someone to meet her.

Every detail was thought out. Now nothing remained but to go to England and act her part, to be kind to an old ailing man, to talk to him about her life—*Myra's* life—and let him see that he was forgiven for all those years of neglect of the little family in Canada.

She was glad she had decided to give herself two days' respite at a hotel.

Vonnie's two air journeys, first across Canada and then from Malton to London Airport, took the edge off her nervousness because she had never flown before and the experience began by being a novelty. But long before she reached England, she grew restless.

When the plane taxied down the runway, she knew the first stirring of real and immediate alarm. She stared out of the window onto the sun and shadow chasing across the great concrete apron and the terminal building and knew that, if she could have, this was the moment when she would have turned and gone back and dismissed as impossible and unforgivable this crazy quixotic thing she was about to do.

But it was too late. She was a long way beyond the point of no return.

The aircraft came to a halt, steps were being wheeled out. Safety belts had been unfastened.

Suppose, at the last minute, someone had come to meet her; suppose over the loud-speaker a voice was already calling her. "Miss Myra Ashlyn . . ."

But no Miss Ashlyn was registered on Flight Number 6. Until she had passed through customs, she was still Yvonne Horne . . . If she heard Myra's name being called, then she would walk through the concourse as though it had no more significance than if it had been Mary Jones.

And then, to the roar of an outgoing plane, her nerves settled. She was expected in two days' time. No one knew that she was already in London so that no one would be paging her over loud-speakers. And if, when she arrived at Uncle Joss's house, she discovered that someone had been sent to meet her, then she could apologize, explain that she had wanted two days in London to "get the feel" of it and that she had not expected to be met.

There was nothing to worry about.

She bent and, pretending to check the locks of her suitcase, ripped off the labels that had her name on and slipped them in her handbag to be torn up and thrown away as soon as she reached the hotel.

"I think of everything!" she thought with a sudden lift of spirits, and walked, as though on wings, out of the airport into the windy sunny morning and the waiting London coach.

The drive into London was not impressive. But then Vonnie had approached too many cities through suburbs to look for anything old or historic on the route.

Her hotel was a quiet one just off Piccadilly. She was shown up to her room on the sixth floor and found, to her delight, that it had a glancing view of the Circus and, over the roofs of buildings, the towers of Westminster pointing up into the sky.

Whatever happened afterwards she was going to enjoy her two solitary days. She unpacked, feverishly impatient to get it over, went down to the hall and bought a guide to London.

Walking down Haymarket, she found St. James's Park. She wasn't aware of being tired after her journey, only of an exhilarating feeling that she was alone in a great city. And then a little thought needled her. This was Nigel's city. . . . She pushed the thought away. It must no longer matter. The past was dead; the future not yet here. There was only the present and that was how she must live until she could completely adjust herself to the thought that she had been hurt like thousands before her and that she must live it down. Then, she could look forward. She saw the twin towers of Westminster Abbey and made for them and, seemingly by a miracle, managed to cross Parliament Square.

She knew that she would go to St. John's Wood that

night. The ordeal of inspecting the house in secret was something that would prey on her mind until she had done it, so best get it over.

The visit was planned because she felt that she should have a knowledge of what the house would be like—a kind of faint, little-girl memory of it. Myra had tried to recall all she could, but Vonnie wanted her own sight of it to augment Myra's memory. This was the only way in which she could make the feeling of the place her own.

She had dinner alone that night in the large dining room of the hotel. Her table was tucked against a wall with a side-view of a paved garden where wrought iron tables stood under bright umbrellas. She lingered over coffee in the lounge, leafing through a magazine, and waited for it to get dark.

The hotel seemed to her to be full of foreigners. She tried to detect their language. French and Italian and German—or was it Dutch? Everyone had cameras and the clerks at the desk in the foyer were being besieged for information. Vonnie had no need of note paper or envelopes or stamps. She must write to no one, lest some little unconsidered thing give her away.

At half past nine she hailed a taxi in Jermyn Street and asked to be taken to the corner of Markyate Avenue in St. John's Wood. She held out some silver to the driver, saying a little helplessly, "Which is half a crown?"

His broad, red kindly face creased into smiles.

"You from Canada, miss?"

"From Vancouver."

"I got a brother who lives in Calgary. You know it?"

"Yes," said Vonnie, warmed by his friendliness. "It's a charming town. You should save up and go out there some time."

He grinned and nodded.

"I'm going when I retire. Going to give meself a real treat!" He gave her change and when she tipped him, he said, "You go around giving two-bob tips for five shilling rides, lady, you'll soon be taking buses!" and handed her back a shilling.

Walking away, Vonnie wondered if there was another city in the world where such a thing would have happened.

Markyate Avenue was wide and lined with plane trees and well-lit. Vonnie peered at the numbers and calculated that No. 10 was about halfway down.

She walked on the far side of the road, watching the houses, taking a note of the numbers on the gates. She felt a little conspiratorial, keeping well to the shadow of the old trees that hung over the tall well-kept fences of the somber Victorian houses, as though she were all set for some dark purpose.

Reaching a house with No. 9 painted on the gatepost she glanced across the road. Ten, then, must be the house with the thick rhododendron hedge and the lamp right outside. She went on a little way, crossed the road and returned, walking past No. 10 twice. There was no light save in the hall, and this, shining through a fan of stained glass, sent only a faint ruby and emerald glow onto the trees.

Vonnie pushed open the gate and was relieved that it moved silently. She slipped into the drive and paused for a moment, listening. There was no sound anywhere, no footsteps on the pavement, no drone of a car engine. The avenue of tall, dignified houses seemed deserted.

Old Joss Ashlyn's home was three-storied with bay windows on either side of the front door. Like all the houses in the road, it stood in its own plot of ground, heavy and dark and frowning. To Vonnie, straight from Canada, it was strange—and typical. A house such as she had seen in pictures, utterly and uncompromisingly Victorian.

She edged her way along the path and because the side windows, too, were in darkness, became bolder.

Myra had said, "Remember about the magnolia tree. Uncle painted my portrait with a background of magnolia flowers. I didn't stay still, of course, and Mother was sitting by to grab me whenever I tried to run away. I only stayed because Uncle promised me a puppy if I did. I never got my poodle pup because we left for Canada soon afterwards."

Vonnie looked around the dark garden and then at the black face of the house. The magnolia tree was clinging to the wall; she could just see the glimmer of white petals.

"And find out if the old swing is still there. You could even remind Uncle of the times he pushed me up and down on it and how I—or *you!*—" her lovely slow smile had broken over her face, "screamed when you went too high!"

Vonnie stood in the shadow of some tall bushes and glanced about her.

The garden was square and surrounded by trees. There seemed to be a great deal of lawn but few flowers. She saw the studio jutting out from the house, with one great wall of window that gaped blackly in the moonless night.

Suddenly a light flashed on in one of the attic rooms. Vonnie darted so abruptly into the bushes that great sprays of leaves brushed across her face with a soft swish that, for a moment, startled her.

Almost immediately, the light went out again.

Myra had said that her uncle had a living-in housekeeper and Vonnie supposed that that was her room.

She turned and went back along the path by the side of the house and when she had nearly reached the short drive again, paused in case whoever had been in the room was on his way out.

A black cat leaned, purring, against her legs. Vonnie, loving cats, but alarmed by its attention at this secret moment, shushed it softly away. The cat's eyes gleamed amber, its tail swished, and it stalked silently into the bushes. Vonnie breathed again and waited, listening for footsteps.

Then she heard the front door open. She pressed back into the bushes, not daring to move forward nearer to the front of the house to see who had come out. She heard quick footsteps on the gravel. There was the clang of the gate as it slammed and then footsteps receded down the road. Somewhere a car door slammed and an engine started up.

Vonnie waited until everything was quiet again, then slipped out of the gate, closing it softly behind her. She walked quickly away from the house towards the lights and traffic of Avenue Road.

At least now she knew what the house looked like; where the studio was; knew that the magnolia clung to the wall; that the house had a low, heavy frame of laurel and rhododendron.

Vonnie slept badly that night and the next. In spite of the fact that she now knew the house, the thought of the ordeal almost upon her was still fraught with doubt. Her emotions swung like a pendulum between self-criticism and self-justification—the two aspects equally strong within her. Tossing and turning in the large, strange bed, she told herself that what she was doing was utterly wrong. Then all the arguments for her coming would sweep over her in a wave of self-exoneration. She was doing this for good reasons—to give Myra her chance of happiness and an old man pleasure towards the end of his life. She was also, she remembered to argue honestly, realizing one of her own dreams to see London. . . .

The whole of the following day passed too swiftly; Vonnie wandered around the West End of London, gazing into shop windows; took taxi rides to famous places; went to a theater in the evening and fell, finally exhausted, into bed, aware that, whatever happened, she had had this day of complete freedom and pleasure to look back on.

The following morning she took a taxi again to St. John's Wood, but this time she had her luggage with her and she was going to drive boldly, as Myra Ashlyn, up to that heavy oak front door.

When the taxi stopped, the driver took her cases for her up the short flight of steps and paused for a moment, giving her a long look. She paid him, thanked him and stood for a moment, panic rising and choking her. She forced her hand to the bell and rang it and waited.

She wished that having rung the bell, like small boys in Vancouver, she could turn and run. But from now on she must fight nerves. She must be self-confident and calm and close her mind to her real identity.

She heard a sound somewhere in the house. Remember you're Myra Ashlyn. Keep saying it. *Myra . . . Myra . . .*

The door swung open.

A tall, very good-looking woman who might have been in her late forties or early fifties stood looking at her, dark brows raised questioningly. She wore a navy dress and pearls around her throat and her dark hair was artistically streaked with white.

Vonnie managed a smile.

"Good afternoon. I'm Miss Ashlyn—"

"Oh, of course! Good afternoon." She held the door open wider. "Please come in." She put out a detaining hand. "And leave your suitcases. I'll see to them."

"But I can carry them!"

"Please!" said the woman and there was polite authority in her voice.

A door to the left of the square hall opened and an old giant of a man came towards her, padding over the parquet floor.

"Myra—my dear!"

Arms reached out and held her strongly: penetrating gray eyes looked down at her. A small, scrupulously kept beard was gray like the great mane of hair.

"Uncle—Joss!"

"This is fine—just fine—and by the way, this is Miss

51

Waring—Rhoda Waring, more my companion than my housekeeper."

The pearls around Rhoda Waring's throat gleamed in the light. She smiled, lifted the suitcases into the hall, and closed the door.

With an arm around Vonnie, old Joss led her into a large bright room with windows looking out onto the garden she had seen in darkness two nights ago.

Sunlight shafted onto two people, a girl and a man, standing together near the window. Vonnie had a swift impression that, as she entered, they had sprung apart. They moved into the center of the room.

"Fenella," old Joss said. "This is Myra. You two cousins haven't met for—what is it—seventeen years!"

The girl called Fenella held out a casual hand; her mouth smiled, but her eyes were quite cold.

"Hello, Myra!"

Vonnie heard herself murmuring politely. At the same time she looked at Fenella Ashlyn in wonder at her beauty. Where Myra was lovely and bright as a tropical flower, Fenella was cool and dark as night. She had nearly black hair fringed lightly over a broad, smooth forehead, and deep blue eyes. Her skin had a faint dark tinge to it, too, as though she used tan make-up. She wore a slim, dark red cotton dress which matched her lipstick.

"You were such little girls when you last met!" old Joss was chuckling, "and whenever I asked you both at the same time to have tea with me, you came and you fought—real fighting, with fists!" He turned to the man. "This, Myra, is Ralph Winslow."

The young man held out his hand with a friendly gesture. Vonnie assessed him with a quick, smiling gaze. He was slim with smooth, brown hair and dark brown eyes. His chin was weak; but his expression was kind.

"The house is too big for me," the old man was explaining, "so I turned the top floor into a flat. Ralph rents it and keeps me company over a Scotch sometimes in the evenings."

Ralph said welcomingly, "I hope you're going to like England."

"As though she'd tell us if she didn't!" Fenella spoke a little too sharply. Her gaze went to Ralph's prolonged grip of Vonnie's hand.

He let go but his smile remained.

"Whether she'd tell us or not isn't important. I still hope she enjoys England."

"I think the circumstances—" Fenella began.

"Let's hope," Joss Ashlyn cut in, "that Myra goes back to Canada glad to have seen London and to have known us."

Vonnie saw the look he gave Fenella. It was full of caution, of warning. Warning of what? A small alarm seemed to sound inside her. She was prepared for a smooth meeting, for everything to be as anticipated. But something in that look warned her that things might be dangerous.

Old Joss was saying,

"Sit down, my dear. I'll get you a sherry. Oh—" he broke off as a black cat jumped from the windowsill and stalked towards them. "Here's another member of my household. His name is Prinny."

"We've got a cat called Gabriel in Vancouver," Vonnie cried. "He's Myr—mine—" she righted herself quickly. She leaned down and stroked him, saying silently to the great, sleek animal. "We've met before, haven't we? Two nights ago. . . ."

Prinny's yellow eyes blinked at her. He stalked to a place in the sun and lay down, flicking his tail.

Vonnie settled back in her chair and felt it enfold her in soft luxury. Everything in the room spelled ease and good taste. The sunlight gave a velvet sheen to the vast, dusky pink Chinese carpet. Lovely lamps stood around; flowers fanned out from two green luster urns; cushions of eau-de-nil silk padded the great settee and the furni-

ture bloomed with a couple of generations of loving polishing. It was an unusual room for an old bachelor, Vonnie thought. Beautiful, gracious even. And then she
realized that she was in England, in an artist's house, and
that all the furniture here was probably handed down
through generations. Some woman—the housekeeper,
perhaps, or Fenella—had probably chosen the cushions
and arranged the flowers.

She was aware suddenly that the brief silence while
old Joss poured out drinks was broken. Fenella was talking, a little too loudly, a little too forcedly, about the
weather.

Vonnie hid a smile. She had heard that when the English were lost for conversation, there was always the
topic of the weather!

But something puzzled her, something about the room
that was not quite right. Or no, not the room, the atmosphere in it. For all its ease and luxury and lovely sunlight, it was overlaid with a strange tension. It linked up
in her mind with the warning look old Joss had given
Fenella only a few minutes ago.

She sat tensely, listening to Fenella's remarks, spoken
in a faintly drawling voice. What had gone wrong? Was
it anything that affected her? Did they know, in ad-
vance, that she was not Myra? Had something happened
to Myra on her way to that holiday in Mexico? And were
they letting her sit there, in ignorance, giving her enough
rein to destroy herself?

"Here you are, my dear!"

Vonnie put up her hand to take the small, cut glass
sherry goblet from the old man and found that her hand
was trembling violently. She managed to set the glass
down on the table by her side and watched him hand
drinks to Fenella and Ralph.

Then he brought his own glass and sat down heavily
in a chair opposite her.

Ralph handed around cigarettes and watched Vonnie
over the flame of his lighter.

Old Joss raised his glass to her. Vonnie reached for hers and managed with an effort to drink without spilling it. The silence was significant. Something had happened. Something was going to be explained at any moment. The fact that she had been welcomed as Myra, kissed as Myra, introduced as Myra, didn't mean a thing. Old Joss was quite capable of saying, "I don't know why you have come here. Or even who you really are. But I do know that you are not Myra. . . ."

He was kindly and charming, but he had strength of character. He wouldn't hesitate to expose her at any moment he chose. . . .

She sat stiff and upright in her chair, drew on her cigarette and received no comfort from it.

Then Joss Ashlyn spoke.

"I had hoped to make this visit an enjoyable one for you."

Vonnie raised her eyes. The gaze of three people was riveted on her. She waited, heart thudding.

"All right," he went on almost angrily, "so I've got a heart condition and the doctors fussed and warned and threatened that I wouldn't live to see the summer out if I didn't do exactly as they told me. Well I fooled them. I got better. That's the best of having a constitution like mine. I'm as well now as I shall ever be—and that's not too bad a state, believe me! In fact, I'm well enough to have taken you out and given you a very nice time, my dear. Only—" he paused and again the heavy silence hung over the room, "only," he repeated, "for the present, at any rate, something has happened to prevent that."

He had spoken gently; he had called her "my dear"; he had looked at her kindly. So, whatever had happened was nothing directly to do with her. She felt a load drop from her and her hand, lifting her sherry glass, was steadier.

"I'm wondering if I'm doing the right thing in keeping you here," he went on. "I don't know! But to send

you away just when you've arrived seems somehow in-
human," he glanced, frowning into his glass. "You didn't
know your Uncle Felix, did you?"

This was a strange new name. Myra hadn't told her!
Alarm struck Vonnie as she shook her head. She had
dreaded the unknown snag that might ruin everything.
And this could be it!

"But of course you didn't. He lived abroad when you
were small—in his young days he was a wanderer and a
drifter. I suppose he was never the proverbial Victorian
black sheep of the family, but he was certainly dark
gray!" He raised his eyes, "Or didn't you meet him once?
I can't quite remember."

Vonnie hesitated, pretending to think. Then she shook
her head.

"Oh, but you did," Fenella said suddenly. "He was
here that day your mother brought you to say good-bye
to Uncle Joss before you left for Canada. I remember
because I was here, too. We were all supposed to be
having a sort of family party and Uncle Felix turned up
unexpectedly. He was a little drunk—"

Old Joss nodded.

"That's what I thought."

"And he began singing some bawdy song at the top
of his voice. Myra and I didn't know what it was all
about, but we loved it," her eyes were narrowed reminis-
cently. "Surely you remember that, Myra, because you
tried to sing it with him and your mother was horrified.
She rounded on Uncle Felix and said it wasn't the sort of
song to sing in front of women and Uncle Felix said
something to the effect that a woman had taught him
that song in a Marseilles bistro and what the hell—?"

"You're making it up," Uncle Joss said. "You were only
seven yourself. You can't remember!"

"Can't I?"

"I'm afraid I was only five at the time and I don't remember it at all."

"Of course you don't! And it's not important, any-

56

way," Joss went on. "But there is something that I have to tell you, something that will be a shock. You're a stranger here, a visitor—"

No one moved. The room was suddenly as still as though it were a painted picture.

"Myra, my dear," said Joss Ashlyn gently, "your Uncle Felix died here two nights ago."

Vonnie didn't speak. Uncle Felix was nothing but a name.

"You might as well know *all* the truth!" Fenella said in a tight husky voice. "He was murdered."

V

SILENCE CLAMPED down once more—the awful, impotent pause of horror when any spoken reaction might sound banal. The ease and security of the room dissolved.

Vonnie said at last in slow horror, "How dreadful! Oh, how dreadful!" She looked from one to the other. Every face was grave but beneath the gravity, each held its own individual significance. Old Joss looked aged and drawn; Fenella's eyes were lowered, her mouth tight; Ralph's gaze, on Vonnie, was guarded and alert as though her reaction interested him more than anything else.

She dragged her eyes from his face.

Fenella broke the heavy silence.

"Let's not be sentimental about it!" she said briefly. "He never bothered about you, Uncle Joss—"

"He was my twin brother."

"I don't think that mattered very much to him until you began to make a lot of money."

"Fenella!"

"Well, it's true! All right, he's dead and he died a horrible way! But he was never any good in his lifetime. He was a sponger and an idler—"

"Whatever he was, he was your uncle—"

"Oh really, Uncle Joss, don't let's wave a banner for the family!" Fenella cried impatiently. She rose with a swift, graceful movement and stood by the mantelshelf sipping her drink. "This is an age of fact-facing. Uncle Felix never did a generous or unselfish thing in his life!"

58

"Let's stop damning the dead," old Joss said quietly.

"But Uncle—"

"Please Fenella," he cut in. "Myra has only just arrived and this is not the time for a family argument. Whatever Felix was, he's dead now so we'll try to think kindly of him. The worst of us have some good in us, somewhere. Now please, let me just tell Myra the facts."

Fenella hunched her shoulders and her eyes flicked to Ralph. But he was still watching Vonnie and she felt a slow flush of embarrassment spread up her throat at the mixture of approval and curiosity in his steady concentrated gaze

"Felix," Joss Ashlyn was saying, "came to see me a few weeks ago. He was penniless and homeless. A man with his qualifications—and he was a highly skilled engineer —should never have been in the state in which he was when he came here. But he had lost jobs through his violent reactionary ways, his inability to accept any discipline, and latterly, his heavy drinking. I hadn't seen him for years, but I couldn't turn him away. The house is large, so I let him have a room providing he kept to himself as much as possible and tried to get a job. He certainly kept to himself—they say twins are alike, but no two could be less alike in character than Felix and I. I saw very little of him although he was in my house, but I am certain he made no attempt to get work. I was to be his keeper for the rest of my life; that's the way he'd planned it and that's the way it was going to be," he shrugged. "Well, I could afford it and, providing he remained out of my way, I didn't mind."

Fenella said quickly, "Can I have another sherry, Uncle Joss?"

"Yes, of course. And you, Myra?"

Vonnie shook her head. She watched Fenella glance at Ralph's glass which was still half full and then cross the room to the drink cabinet.

With her back to them, she said in the same taut voice, "I'm sorry if I interrupted, Uncle Joss. But do go on."

Vonnie looked at the raven-dark bent head, the sweep of neckline to slender shoulders, the red silk rippling over the straight back as she lifted the sherry bottle.

"I know how you feel," Joss said. "How you must be hating this, my dear. But Myra must hear the story. "He turned to her again. "The night before last I went out to dinner with an old friend. I'd seen Felix in the morning and he said he hadn't felt well. He was going to bed early. I told Rhoda to keep an eye on him. She went to his room later in the afternoon and he was sitting reading and seemed cheerful enough.

"She was going out that night, too, to see friends, but she said that if I liked, she'd stay and get Felix a meal. I told her not to stay in, but to take something cold up to him on a tray. When I came home that evening I did what I always do last thing at night—I looked in the studio to see that the door to the garden was locked. I turned on the light—" he paused, set down his glass and leaned forward, clasping his hands between his knees, "and Felix was lying on the floor. He was dead."

"But," Fenella said, carrying her drink back to her chair, "no one dreamed at first that it was murder. He hadn't been shot, or knifed or strangled—"

Vonnie sat staring at them, three strangers telling her of a murder.

"To all outward appearances," old Joss said, "Felix died of a stroke. But there were bruises, dreadful, enormous bruises everywhere. I thought at first that they were caused somehow by his falling and that the shock of the fall had brought on a stroke."

"But it wasn't like that," Fenella said slowly, "and the awful thing was that Uncle found him! The shock of that could have killed him. If only Rhoda or Ralph had come in first—"

"If I had been the first home," Ralph said defensively, "I wouldn't have gone near your uncle's studio. I'd have gone straight to my own flat. Rhoda, of course, might have looked in to check the windows."

"But—" Vonnie began, "who—killed him?"

Old Joss shook his head.

"So far there have been no clues. All we know is that someone came to this house two nights ago, while everyone was out. Probably a stranger."

Two nights ago! Vonnie heard no more of what Joss Ashlyn was saying. She was thinking, in sick fear, *two nights ago I was here, in the garden*. . . . Perhaps someone from one of the houses nearby saw me, watched me go, saw my face in the lamplight outside the house so clearly that he could recognize me . . . *I was here!* . . . and behind the great dark studio windows at which she had stood staring, a man had probably already lain dead or dying. . . .

She brushed her hand across her forehead, feeling its heat and the sudden throbbing at her temples.

Joss watched her.

"I'm sorry to have to tell you all this. You're not involved, but the very fact that you are in this house might mean that the police could want to see you."

"But Myra wasn't here when it happened!" Ralph protested.

"I know, but the C.I.D. have a way of turning over every stone. Oh, they won't worry you, my dear, once they check on your day of arrival in this country," he smiled at her.

Vonnie stared back at him in horrified dismay.

Once they checked on her, they would find out that she had arrived two days ago, that she was not Myra Ashlyn. All right, so they would discover her masquerade! But that wouldn't mean that she would be suspected of murder. As herself, Vonnie Horne, she was even less suspect since she was neither related to nor had she ever known Felix Ashlyn . . . As Vonnie Horne, no emotion or grievance against any of the Ashlyn family could whip her to the mad destruction of one of them!

Discovery of what she had done, however, would mean further shock for this keen, handsome old man, distress for Myra and shame for herself. Since no one could be expected to believe her motives, she would be seen as an irresponsible adventuress, or even someone out for financial gain.

Joss Ashlyn was covering up her long, shocked silence by an explanation as to how his brother had died.

"There are devilish ways to murder, Myra. This one was, in its way, unusual. It all hung on a physical idiosyncrasy which Felix and I, being twins, share." He paused.

Vonnie glanced up from her taut contemplation of her locked hands and saw Ralph standing over her, offering cigarettes. She took one, no longer trying to hide the shaken nerves that made her hands tremble. Ralph seemed to understand. He snapped open his lighter and put it to her cigarette and then with his other hand, steadied hers. As she leaned away, drawing on her cigarette, she saw Fenella's blue, contemplating gaze on her. She said, "Thank you," briefly to Ralph and was careful not to look at him.

"I keep a bottle of brandy in my studio," Joss was saying, "and Felix must have prowled around the house whenever I was out and in the last few days come upon the bottle and helped himself lavishly. The police doctor thinks he can only have found this bottle maybe two or three days before he died. It was full when I put it in the cupboard and practically empty when the police discovered it. At some time or other someone had added a drug to that bottle—"

"Poison?" Vonnie whispered.

"Oh no," the old man shook his head. "That's just the strange part of it. There is a drug sometimes used as a sedative that has a urea derivative," he paused. "It's harmless in nine hundred and ninety-nine cases out of a thousand, but I'm that thousandth. I am, in fact, so allergic that a few doses would be fatal."

"And that—that drug was in the brandy?"

He nodded.

"It's a very rare allergy that affects the platelets in the blood, destroys them and the result has a kind of hemophiliac effect. When I saw the great bruises on Felix's skin, I didn't give it a thought. It was years since I'd taken the drug for sleeping purposes and in those days it was on the medical free list. Now it can be taken only on doctor's orders. I bought it over the counter, took it on three consecutive nights and it nearly killed me. It's so long ago that I'd forgotten the incident. As my twin it's pretty reasonable to conclude that Felix must have been allergic too. At any rate, the doctor says he must have taken brandy from this bottle over the past two or three days and the final dose killed him. He wouldn't have guessed in a thousand years what was wrong with him—you don't have pain, you see, only these great warning bruises, larger than—oh, far larger than—my hand." He spread out his hands and looked at them.

"If he had been found earlier," Fenella said, "his life might have been saved."

"The doctor would have forbidden him to move an inch. He would have had to lie flat and inert for probably three days—that is the time it takes the platelets in the body to form again and he would have quickly become as fit as he was before. But he must have moved about and so caused cerebral hemorrhage and his own death."

"But Uncle Joss—it's dreadful!" Vonnie was unaware of the fact that, in her dismay, she had quite naturally used the name she had thought would be so difficult, "Uncle Joss."

He glanced at her unhappily.

"You see it's not a happy household, my dear, and it won't be for the next few days with the police around! So, if you like, I'll find you a nice hotel to stay in. I'll understand. In your place, I'd want to get away myself."

Vonnie sat tightly in her chair. Joss Ashlyn was offering her a reprieve. It would be so much safer to stay somewhere away from the house and just come here for visits, so much easier to be on guard for part of the day rather than have to watch herself every moment. Besides, if she left at once, perhaps the police would not question her. . . .

She looked at the old man and words of gratitude and acceptance of his suggestion formed.

"I—" she began. And then quite suddenly she knew that whatever the risk to herself, she couldn't go. One of her reasons for coming here was to please old Joss. If she crawled away and hid, shuddering and scared in some hotel, she would lose a great part of her self-justification in coming here. And if she did that, her whole effort would lose its meaning. She must not default from the price she had to pay for coming here, not even for her own sake. She saw the pleading in the old man's eyes as he looked at her and knew that, if she went away and hid, she would despise herself for the rest of her life. Whatever happened, she must stay and see this thing through. It wasn't blind courage or sentiment; it was that far stronger thing—a feeling of being right with herself.

"It's a struggle for you, isn't it," Joss said. "You don't want to hurt my feelings by going. But I won't be hurt. You're young and you're a stranger here. We have no right to hold you in a murder house."

"No! No, Uncle Joss," she heard her own voice carry clearly across the quiet, waiting room. "I haven't the slightest intention of leaving now that I'm here. If you really want me to stay, then of course, I'll stay with you. Why not? I'm not involved."

She thought someone in the room gave a faint gasp. Relief? Dismay? She glanced from Fenella to Ralph and back again. Neither was looking at her, yet she was aware of the increased tension in the room.

Joss Ashlyn's expression, however, was compensation for everything. She had thrown away her chance of a reprieve—and, in that wild emotional moment, she didn't care.

"Thank you, Myra. I'll do all I can to see that you're kept out of the unpleasantness. After all, you weren't in England when it happened," he smiled at her. "And perhaps it will all be over soon and then I can make up to you for this rather dreadful arrival."

Vonnie asked as quietly as she could, "Weren't there any clues, Uncle Joss? Surely—"

"No clues," he shook his head, "because no one knows exactly when the drug was put into the brandy bottle. No one except myself has been in the studio for weeks—in fact, since long before I put that bottle there in case I needed it."

"Except," said Fenella, "Little Woody and, of course, Rhoda."

"Little Woody," Joss explained, "is the rather simple girl we have to do the rough work. She gets her nickname through her thick, wooden expression. She's simple, but she's good. And Rhoda—well, of course, she goes in there to dust, but Rhoda wouldn't kill."

Fenella asked huskily, "How do you know that?"

"As well as I know that you couldn't have done this thing," he said quietly.

They all looked at Ralph as he rose, saying calmly, "We can only guess that someone who had a grudge against Fenella's uncle followed him here and broke into the house one evening."

"Certainly no one came during the day! Rhoda would have seen or heard him. Besides which, I spend a lot of my time there. Since I've given up portrait painting, I've taken up a hobby. I work in stained glass. It's a fascinating pastime."

"It's almost become a new profession, hasn't it," Uncle Joss?" Fenella remarked. "In fact, you've given up one art form to take another."

He smiled.

"But I don't take money for the work I do. Occasionally I give a window to some place which needs stained glass work and can't afford to pay. I'd nearly completed a panel for a rebuilt church in a particularly poor part of London. When Felix fell, he knocked against it and smashed it. Glass was everywhere and only the leads remained intact."

Ralph said, "I saw it just as it was nearing completion. All that fine work ruined!"

"The report of the murder was in all the newspapers," Fenella said, "complete with reproductions of some of Uncle's most famous portraits."

If she had bothered to read the English newspapers during the past two days, Vonnie would have seen it all. Would she still have come here, or would she have fled back to Canada? Now she knew why the taxi man had shot her that strange look when she had given him the address. She had been going to a house of a violent death; she, a young thing who, even on her second taxi ride here, hadn't known a half-crown from a florin!

She sat quite still, watching the cat flick his tail at a fly.

"Greta, the German maid in the house next door, was looking out of her window and told the police she saw someone in Uncle's garden. She says she was sure it was a woman and that she seemed to be peering about her as though looking for a way in."

Ralph's words cut across Vonnie's thoughts. Hot and cold waves of alarm began to shiver through her.

"She says whoever the woman was, she kept well in the shadows—"

"And the time coincided with that at which Uncle Felix died. Greta said she knows exactly what time it was because she was just going to meet her boyfriend and they were going to the German Club."

"It's possible that she's making the story up," Joss said.

"Why should she?"

The first spontaneous laugh of that strange, tense session burst from Ralph.

"She's rather lovely, like a miniature Brunnehilde—and she has dreams of a stage career. Maybe she thinks if she can get a hearing over this affair someone will publish her photograph in the newspapers and she'll be snapped up by some company and groomed for film stardom."

"*You* may think she's attractive," Fenella said sharply, "but wait for another five years—she'll be fat and floppy with all the sausages she probably eats and the ale she drinks at that German Club—"

"I think we won't discuss the merits or demerits of the maid next door," Josh Ashlyn said quietly.

"I'm sorry, Uncle," Fenella said instantly. Her beautiful face softened as she smiled at him. "But I'm inclined to believe Greta's story. I've already told you what I think. Someone had a grudge against Uncle Felix and followed him here and waited and watched for his—or her—opportunity. And Greta could have been wrong; it could have been a man. If he kept close to the bushes at the side of the fence, then it would be difficult to be certain on a dark night."

"But how could a stranger have got into the house to dope the brandy, in the first place?"

Fenella looked at Ralph as though his question was the ultimate stupidity.

"Isn't that obvious? He, or she, could have waited until everyone else was out—and Rhoda seems to take any evening off she likes. You spoil her, Uncle Joss! Then, whoever killed Uncle Felix could have merely knocked on the door and been let in by him. Whoever called could even have pretended to be a friend—have even been looked upon by Uncle Felix as one!"

"And how?" old Joss asked, gray eyebrows lifted, "could whoever called have got into the studio?"

"Uncle Felix could have taken him in there—"

"Why, if I was out and the drawing room was empty?"

"I don't know—" Fenella sought in her mind, frowned thoughtfully at the old man and said, "Suppose Uncle Felix was afraid you'd come back soon and didn't want the lights to be seen on in the drawing room, so he took whoever called into the studio? After all, it's at the back of the house and he'd have ample opportunity, as soon as he heard your footsteps in the hall, to bundle his visitor out through the studio door into the garden."

"Always supposing the visitor was prepared to be bundled," Ralph said. "But go on."

Fenella's gaze rested on him for a silent moment. Vonnie, watching, thought: Does she love him? Or hate him? The look was intense enough for either emotion.

"Well, perhaps whoever called was offered a drink and he—or she—knew Uncle Felix's weakness for brandy but decided to ask for something else for himself. Perhaps he went into the dining room to fetch whisky or gin and that was the murderer's opportunity. There was the bottle of brandy brought from the cupboard and put on the table. The visitor already knew of Uncle Joss's allergy and guessed that, as a twin, Uncle Felix would suffer from the same thing. It was perhaps just a chance and he—took it." She ended on a little note of triumph, her beautiful, elongated eyes glancing from one to the other, and finally coming to rest, narrowing a little, on Vonnie.

It was old Joss Ashlyn who spoke. He rose, walked with his heavy, bear-like tread across the room and opened a French window that led out onto a small verandah and down some steps into the garden.

Staring out at the bright afternoon, hands behind his back, he said, "It's a theory, Fenella, and in a way, a feasible one. But on the other hand, there were surely more certain ways of killing Felix. It would have been pure conjecture that he, too, would have this allergy."

"It was very probable, though," Ralph said. "Twins share the same blood, the same alchemy."

"But surely he knew that you had the allergy?"

"He was somewhere abroad when I went into the hospital and we never corresponded."

Joss sighed, turned and faced them. His back was to the light and he looked like some gigantic shadow against the bright green of the garden outside.

"I'm afraid I'm inclined to the theory the police are working on. The drink wasn't meant for Felix, but for me! Someone knew I kept a bottle of brandy there. Only, I seldom take a drink in the studio. In fact, I'd almost forgotten I had a bottle there and Felix found it and the wrong man was killed."

"Oh no!" Fenella cried, and her hand moved involuntarily as though to push the thought away. "Uncle Joss, no! I won't believe that anyone wanted to harm *you*. I can't—"

"Let's stop talking about it, shall we?" the old man said briskly, "because anything we say is only conjecture. I've a great faith in the British police, let's leave it to them."

"But Uncle, suppose—suppose whoever tried—tries again. Suppose—"

"I'll have to watch my step, won't I?" He spoke with a touch of jocularity, but his face was grave. "Well, I have no intention of dying before my time, so don't worry. Now, Fenella, I think Myra should be shown her room. We've brought her here and plunged her straight into our troubles! She must want to collect herself, get her bearings and unpack. If—that is—you really mean you want to stay."

"I really mean it," Vonnie said quietly, and rose.

He watched her, smiling a little.

"You have the same room you slept in as a little girl. wonder if you remember?"

"It was a long time ago, Uncle Joss."

He had moved to the mantelshelf and had picked up small bronze statuette of a child, head thrown back, laughing.

"Do you remember how you used to love to play with this?"

Vonnie hesitated and then gave a cautious nod.

Fenella's eyes flashed around at her.

"I don't know how you can remember *that!*" her voice was clear and challenging, "because it was *I* who used to play with that statuette. I used to call her 'Starlina' after some fairy in a pantomime I'd seen."

Vonnie stood quite still, a smile set on her face, her heart thudding with the alarming realization of how easy it was going to be to make slips, to remember wrongly, which was far worse than not remembering at all.

"Myra was pandering to an old man's bad memory!" Joss Ashlyn said. "Run along, my dear, and get down to your unpacking."

Run along . . . and be very careful, because if you make a mistake, you aren't going to escape! Fenella was watching and she'd pounce. She was quick and too many errors would start the seeds of suspicion in her alert mind. . . .

VI

THE GUEST ROOM was old-fashioned and charming. Green and white chintz brightened the heavy antique furniture; there were pink, sweet-smelling stocks in a small white vase and a view from the open window of the garden.

Vonnie rested her hands on the sill and looked down and saw the magnolia climbing the wall to the left of her window.

"I didn't dream you had such lovely weather in England!" she said genuinely surprised. "I'd always heard it rained a lot."

"It does," Fenella said. "But you've arrived in freak weather. It happens sometimes—a heat wave in May. And we *have* been known to have snow in June, so don't be too thrilled about it all!" She gave a short laugh. "And now for the geography of the house. The bathroom is just opposite and Rhoda's room is next door."

"Rhoda's attractive, isn't she?"

Fenella's eyes were veiled. She was half-heartedly arranging the flowers, fanning them out.

"If you like the *femme fatale* type. Yes."

"Has she been with Uncle long?"

"Some years."

"I thought she was a friend—a guest in the house, when I first saw her. She dresses so well and I always imagined housekeepers to be elderly and brisk!"

"Oh, Rhoda's an enigma," Fenella broke off a brown pitted leaf, leaned across Vonnie, tossing it out of the window. It fluttered on the light air to the path. "Nobody really knows much about her." She stopped fidgeting with the flowers and leaned against the tallboy, folding her arms. Her brilliant eyes regarded Vonnie with amusement. In that moment there was a look of Myra about her, a kind of dancing mischief. But the bright generous planes of Myra's face were missing. Fenella's mischief had malice in it.

"There was a sort of hint going around seven years ago, when Rhoda first came, that she was an old flame of Uncle Joss. I don't know how true that is. None of us knows her any better now than when she first came. She never talks about herself though I'm perfectly certain she's had a rich and exciting past. She's got that look. It's odd that she's content to live here with an old man."

"Perhaps he'll marry her?"

Fenella laughed aloud.

"No woman ever caught Uncle Joss and most certainly no woman will do so now!" Her eyes grew speculative. "I've often wondered whether *she* knew Uncle Felix and whether she really *was* out on the night he was killed!"

"You're not suggesting that Rhoda—"

"Murdered him? Good heavens, whatever *I* think, I don't share it with anyone!" The already familiar closed look came over her face. "I'm not brandishing my suppositions only, perhaps, to find an action for slander entered against me!"

Vonnie moved away from the window.

Suppose I said, "But someone was here that night because I saw a light flick on and off in one of the attic rooms. . . ." But I don't dare! I don't dare involve myself. . . . She shivered.

"What's the matter?" Fenella was watching her.

Vonnie said, "It's all so horrible."

"It is," Fenella agreed. Her arms were crossed, her fingers dug at silken arms. "That's why I'm surprised you chose to stay when you were given the chance of escaping. A house where there's been a murder—"

"I came all this way just to see Uncle Joss," Vonnie

said quietly, "and I intend to stay. He wants me to—I could see that."

"How very unselfish of you!" But the way Fenella said it made a mockery of the word.

"Not altogether," Vonnie's voice was as cool as Fenella's. "Unselfishness can be an indulgence, can't it? You want to please someone because it pleases you to give him happiness? You want to feel good with yourself!"

Fenella said irritatedly, "That's all too deep for me! Oh, well, if you want to endure a house of police and detectives and newspaper men, that's your affair!"

Vonnie asked, "You don't live here?"

"Me? Good heavens, no! I've got a flat just around the corner. But I come here a lot—Uncle Joss likes me to. And then, of course, there's Ralph. I introduced him to Uncle."

"Oh."

"And it works very well. Ralph has the top floor—"

The attic rooms! And someone was there in the room that looked onto the garden on the night the house was supposed to be empty, save for a man dying downstairs in the studio. . . .

Fenella stirred and glanced down at Vonnie's two suitcases. They were smart and modern; one was of a dark red composition material with the initials "M.A." stamped in the corner.

"They're American, aren't they?" Fenella asked.

"Yes."

"Luggage over there is so much smarter than ours!" she said reluctantly. "If ever I can manage to visit the States, luggage will be one of my main 'buys.' You're very lucky living so near New York!"

Vonnie said in genuine surprise, "But I live thousands of miles away! Vancouver is right on the other side of the continent and Seattle is our nearest American city."

"My geography!" Fenella mourned. "It's a good thing I don't have to use it in my job! If I did I'd soon be sitting, on the curb, hand outstretched, crying to passers-by, 'Alms for the love of Allah!"

"I don't even know what your job is," Vonnie ventured

"I work in a photographic studio. Mostly I cope with spoiled rich women, or bored models."

"In spite of that," Vonnie said, "it sounds interesting." Fenella shot her an unfriendly look.

"You can have it! It's ninety percent boring."

"What work would you like to do?"

"None at all!" Fenella said frankly.

"Well, that's honest, at any rate!" Vonnie laughed.

"I first met Ralph through my job. He's an advertising man."

Vonnie said, because a comment was obviously expected of her, "Oh? He's nice, isn't he?"

Fenella didn't say a word. She just raised her eyes and something in that steady, almost cat-like stare sent an unmistakable message to Vonnie. It said as clearly as though she had shouted the words: *Keep away! Ralph belongs to me!*

Vonnie changed the subject, saying vaguely, "I suppose I'd better unpack—"

"Yes. But there's no need to hurry over it. Take all the time you want. Lunch isn't until a quarter past one."

"You're staying for it?"

"Oh yes." Fenella gave a short laugh. "I almost always lunch with Uncle Joss on a Saturday. It's a kind of ritual. Unless, of course, I have some special 'date.' In fact, I'm here a great deal since Uncle's illness. He likes me around. We're very close, you know."

"I'm glad. He'd have been lonely otherwise—"

"Oh, he's got masses of friends and—" she added, "it seems one enemy! But all my life I've come to look on this house as a sort of real home. And this past few weeks, since he had his first heart attack, my flat is just where I sleep and eat sometimes and have parties. Ralph very often joins us for meals, too. He and Uncle get on splendidly. I'm glad. It's just what I'd hoped for," she wandered to the door. "I'd better leave you to your unpacking."

She paused on the threshold and said, half over her shoulder, "It is rather a farce to say I hope you'll enjoy your stay. With all this horror going on around us, I doubt if you will. But well—*you've* chosen to stay!"

The door closed softly and Vonnie was alone.

Fenella's last words seemed to echo around the charming room as though somewhere there was a warning in them. A warning of what? That she most certainly wasn't going to enjoy herself? That, in fact, Fenella hoped she wouldn't? There had seemed to be that inference, too, in her voice. And Vonnie knew, without a doubt, that however hard she tried and however long she stayed, Fenella Ashlyn would never more than tolerate her. . . .

She wandered around the room, touching things. She had always been like this, she thought, amusement relaxing her face—wanting to touch objects, to feel them almost as though she received more contact with them that way than by sight, like a blind person. She ran her fingers along the highly polished surface of the tallboy, stroked the heavy ornate drawer handles, felt the soft green and white sprigged chintz of the bedcover and liked the soft, satiny finish.

The room was charming and feminine with the green silk cushion on the bed, the flowers and the picture on the wall.

Vonnie stood gazing up at it.

It was a fine seascape and her heart gave a small lurch. It could have been painted from Vancouver Island, looking out over the Pacific. The gold and violet reflected in the bright water brought a shock of memory to her. Out of the immediate past, Nigel seemed to cross her vision, to be here in the room. She took a swift, involuntary step back as though to avoid walking into him. Nigel . . . Oh no, not the memory of him here! Not the thing from which she had hoped to escape, brought back into her life by one lovely seascape on a strange wall!

Her fingers began to itch to turn the picture face to the wall. She swung herself quickly away. This was absurd! The seascape could have been painted anywhere. Somewhere in England or Scotland. It had no link with Vancouver save in her imagination. Surely she had enough to think about and guard against without a voluntary resurrection of a love affair that was over almost before it had started! . . .

She turned to her suitcases, unlocked them and began to shake out dresses and hang up suits; she laid blouses and underclothes in the deep, fragrant drawers that held a scent she did not recognize. After this visit, for the rest of her life, whenever she smelled the rose and musk of potpourri, she would be reminded of this room in St. John's Wood.

It was characteristic of Vonnie to move quietly. When she had changed into a cool pink and gray candy-striped dress, had done her hair and put on large gray pearl earrings, she opened her door and went along the passage with its thick dark red pile carpet.

The staircase swept in a curve to the hall and, rounding the bend, hand on the banister, she saw Ralph standing quite still outside the closed door of the drawing room. His head was near the paneling in an attitude of listening and his right hand rested lightly on the wall. There was no indication from his manner that he was about to enter the room. Only that he was intent upon hearing the conversation that was being carried on inside.

Vonnie quickened her pace down the staircase, letting her heels thud here and there on the woodwork to announce her coming. She saw Ralph start, straighten and half turn. Then he opened the door and went in.

Vonnie heard him say, briskly, "I hope I'm not too early, sir."

And old Joss replied, "Of course you're not! Come on

in. Lunch is ready and we'll have it as soon as Myra is down."

"I'm here," she walked in, smiling at the old man who was sitting with the cat crouched, like a witch's "familiar," on his shoulder.

"Do you remember your bedroom, Myra?" he asked.

"I'm afraid I don't," she said cautiously.

"Well, that's not surprising. I never quite trust these people who can remember the color of the winter coat they had when they were three! And, anyway, the room's changed quite a bit. That's Rhoda's doing," he chuckled.

Fenella's eyes flicked to Vonnie.

"Rhoda says we want new curtains or a new carpet, and Uncle *has* new curtains or carpets! For a house-keeper, she certainly bosses you, Uncle Joss!"

He said, unperturbed, "Since I've spent my life concentrating on my work, it's necessary for someone to do that! No creative artist should be bothered with chores —and most certainly not a man! I come from the old school which likes to see a woman around, being decorative *and* useful in the kitchen."

"In other words, Uncle Joss, you belong to the kitchen sink club!" Fenella said.

"I'm not up on modern jargon, I don't know what you mean," he said a little testily.

"Don't worry," Fenella crossed around the back of his chair, leaned over him and patted his shoulder. "I was only teasing you."

She could not resist baiting him, but immediately afterwards she was sorry. Because in that well-hidden heart of hers she loved him? Vonnie wondered, and was not convinced. Instinct told her that Fenella Ashlyn did nothing without personal motive.

There were light footsteps outside and Rhoda entered.

"Lunch is ready when you are."

"Coming now," Joss said.

"I'll come and help you," Fenella said.

"Thank you, but it's not necessary," Rhoda flashed back, and went out. Fenella followed her, pausing at the door to say, "We always have this argument. But Rhoda knows quite well that I'll help. She likes to think I pay in service for the food she provides for me."

As her sharp little heels tapped along the passage, Joss said, "Those two have never hit it off; I suppose certain types of people—particularly women—have an instinctive mistrust of one another."

Vonnie said, bridling and teasing, "Why only women, Uncle Joss. Men, too—"

He shot her an amused glance.

"All right, have it your way! Men, too!" He got up, slipped a heavy arm around her shoulders. "Come along and let's eat. You know, when a man reaches my age, however disinterested he's been in his vigorous youth over food, he gets a kind of childish pleasure out of the thought of what he's going to eat. Come, Ralph."

Old Joss sat at the head of the mahogany table, beautifully laid out with embroidered mats, cut glass and deep yellow hothouse roses in a low center bowl. Rhoda sat facing him at the far end. With the sheen of the pearls against her soft, still-young throat and her shapely head outlined against the sunlight, she looked far more the hostess than the housekeeper.

Vonnie sat next to Joss with Fenella and Ralph opposite.

The sliced avocados in the small glass dishes had center fillings of pale pink shrimps; the rolls, covered by a white napkin, were hot; the butter was shaped into little Tudor roses. Everything, Vonnie thought when the cold turkey and salad was served, was beautifully prepared and perfectly served. Whether or not the handsome, silent Rhoda had been one of Uncle Joss's "old flames," she certainly knew how to produce a delicious lunch.

Joss asked Vonnie about her life in Canada. That was

easy to answer. She could describe it as she and Myra lived it, only putting herself in Myra's place as head of the secretarial bureau.

"And this friend you share your flat with?" he asked. "Vonnie?"

"Yes. Yvonne Horne. Our parents were neighbors when we first went to live in Vancouver; then they became friends and so did we. We went to the same college together, went on the same skiing parties in the mountains, swam and sailed together in the summer."

"Is she attractive?"

Vonnie hesitated and laughed.

"She's—ordinary. But we get on well."

"And both of you are around the same age! Twenty-five, isn't it? And neither of you married yet."

"No, not yet, Uncle Joss."

"Well, I don't know Yvonne, but where you're concerned, the men are certainly slow!" His keen eyes appraised her and she felt the color rise in her throat. "Don't go sticking together too much, you two, and becoming a couple of old maids! Can't abide old maids!"

At the end of the table Rhoda dropped a spoon. Vonnie glanced at her. Her face was still very pale but her eyes were bright and angry. She gave Joss a long, strange look.

"Old maids, as you call them," she said steadily, "are forced into that position by men."

Joss was unperturbed. He grinned at her.

"*Touché!*" he said, chuckling silently.

But Rhoda was angry. Lunch was over and she pushed back her chair and rose, gathering plates, moving with a quiet dignity, holding her curious, secret anger on a tight rein.

"I'll bring the dishes out," Fenella called after her.

"Thank you."

Fenella stood, smoothing her dress over her slender thighs.

"You know, Uncle Joss, how sensitive she is about that

subject. You shouldn't—you really *shouldn't!* Anyway, if you had made an honest woman of her—"

A great hand crashed on the table; the silver and the glass rattled.

"That's quite enough!" Joss's shaggy eyebrows came down so low that they almost hid his eyes. "You take too much on yourself when you speak like that!"

Fenella went a little white.

"I'm sorry, Uncle Joss. It was only a joke. I mean, I—"

"Whatever you meant, don't do it again!" He pushed back his chair. "Rhoda is, and always ever has been, merely my housekeeper. She came in answer to an advertisement I put in a newspaper seven years ago and I thank heaven for her. One more such impertinence from you, and you can take your meals in your own flat. Is that clear?"

"Yes, Uncle Joss, I said I'm sorry, I didn't think!"

"Oh yes you did! You must guard your tongue, Fenella."

She said in a small voice, "Yes, Uncle Joss."

"And don't make slanderous statements. Rhoda came here as my housekeeper. Before that, I never knew her."

Fenella stood, hands clutching the back of her chair. The look of contrition on her face vanished as he stalked out of the room.

"And that, darling Uncle Joss," she said softly, "is the lie of your life!"

"Fenella, stop it!" Ralph cried sharply.

She looked across the room at him. "I shouldn't have said it, I suppose. But really, for Uncle Joss to play at righteous indignation is just too much! I said what I did as one sophisticate to another. And it's true, you know, because I remember years ago hearing my mother talking about Uncle's latest *amour*—a model called Rhoda."

"Well, there could be more than one Rhoda."

Fenella gave him a savage look.

"If you doubt me, I'll give you proof. One of these days, when all this horrible business of Uncle Felix's murder is over and Uncle Joss is out, I'll take you into the studio and show you a whole dusty collection of Uncle Joss's old paintings, portraits and things. Most of them are unfinished preliminaries he did before he began his real canvas. But there are one or two—and one in particular of Rhoda when she was young.

"It could be someone like her."

"But it isn't," Fenella said softly, "because she's wearing a sort of green shawl and pinned on her shoulder is that curious gold Pan's head brooch she often wears. So you see—"

"Ssh—ssh—" Ralph hissed.

Rhoda was coming back.

Fenella moved to the side table and began gathering up dishes.

Vonnie collected unused cutlery, asking, "Where do I put these?"

Silently Fenella opened a drawer in an old-fashioned sideboard.

Rhoda had brought in a tray. She piled plates from the sidetable on them.

"Will you be here for dinner this evening, Fenella?" she asked.

"No—" Fenella began and turned to Ralph. "We're going into town, aren't we, to see that film?"

Ralph said diffidently, "I don't think we should. Not in view of—"

"For heaven's sake, we're not involved in Uncle Felix's death! We can't be expected to sit at home waiting for someone to be arrested!"

"Nevertheless, I think we *should* stay around," Ralph said, "just for the next day or two. The film you want to see will run for some time yet. We'll go next week."

Fenella glanced out of the window.

"Then I'll go to the flat and change into a sun dress and come back. On a hot afternoon like this, I think Uncle Joss's garden is the best place to be. Myra, I expect you'd like to relax, too, after your air journey—"

"It sounds like a lovely idea," she said evasively.

"And Rhoda," Fenella said to the tall figure in the doorway, "don't bother to stay in to get tea for Uncle Joss. I'll be here; I'll see to it."

Rhoda said quietly, "Oh, but I intend to stay in! There's a symphony concert Mr. Ashlyn and I want to listen to." She addressed her remark to Fenella without even looking around. Still with the graciousness of a hostess, she carried the loaded tray to the kitchen.

Fenella said in a low voice, "You see how she stakes her claim on Uncle Joss? And I'll bet when none of us is around she doesn't call him 'Mr. Ashlyn'!"

Ralph turned and grinned at Vonnie.

"Take no notice! She's always needling about Rhoda. Not that it makes the least difference to her. She's the calmest person I've ever seen."

"Except when Uncle Joss referred to 'old maids'!" Fenella snapped.

He reached out and flicked lightly at her face.

"Stop it, sweet!" he said softly, "you don't look very pretty when you're being catty."

"I'm sorry," she gave him a brilliant smile. "But I don't like her—and I never shall."

"But your uncle does. And that's all that really matters, isn't it?"

"I think," Fenella said as though she couldn't leave the subject alone, "that's all that matters to her, too!"

She walked past Vonnie and out of the room.

Ralph said, "Don't take any notice. Fenella doesn't mean half she says! It's a pose."

But, thought Vonnie, putting away unused cutlery, Fenella *did* mean it; she meant every word. In fact, she meant far more than she said! She hated Rhoda Waring. . . .

VII

THEY SAT in the garden after lunch. The sky was nearly cloudless and the birds searched boldly for food about their feet. Fenella went to her flat and returned an hour later wearing a beautifully cut white sun dress and carrying an armful of magazines. Old Joss dozed. Fenella dumped the magazines on a wrought iron table and said, "Help yourself, Myra."

But, for all the peace and inertia of the afternoon, there was a sensation of unrest. Vonnie guessed why. From the houses around, people might be watching them through the trees, curious about the people in this house of murder. Who did it? Which one? Joss Ashlyn? Fenella? Ralph? Rhoda Waring? Or a stranger?

And at any moment the police might call or the telephone ring. Rhoda had instructions not to admit reporters; but Joss had told Vonnie that the rush of them was over now. That had occurred during the day after the murder. Now they had as much of the story as was known and all that remained was go await the unraveling of the affair by the police.

After tea, Vonnie went to her room to finish unpacking. Fenella stayed in the garden with Joss who had returned there after listening to the concert.

When she had finished, she stacked her suitcases away and went and sat on the window seat. She could just see Joss Ashlyn's stretched out legs and Fenella's slim feet in green sandals. She looked around at the houses at the end of the garden. A wall of trees separated them but through those leafy branches, she was quite sure that people wandered to their own windows to gaze into the garden because there weren't many who could resist the intrigue of murder.

Vonnie leaned back, hands in her lap, relieved to be alone and to face the fact that she had been offered, and had refused, freedom from the strain that she would obviously feel in this house. Some strong, almost filial sense, had prompted her to stay. She had known old Joss Ashlyn only half an hour when she had had to make her decision. Myra had said he had been selfish; he had cared nothing for the welfare of her parents or herself once they had left for Canada. On the face of it, Myra had been justified for her outburst of bitterness when the letter came inviting her to England. But there was most certainly something about this old giant of a man that drew a kind of reluctant affection and a desire to make excuses for his action. After all, there could have been some good reason for the way he had ignored Myra's family. There might even have been a quarrel between the families of which Myra had been told nothing. Whatever the reason, the fact remained that from that first instant of meeting Joss, from that moment when he had laid his arm around her shoulder and drawn her into their lives, she had capitulated to the old man's charm.

The hot afternoon made her drowsy. Her eyes were closed, her thoughts swinging in that relaxed state between sleeping and waking, when a knock on her door startled her. She shot from her chair, asking sharply, "Who is it?"

Ralph's voice outside, said, "I've been sent to tell you that the police are here again."

Vonnie stood for a moment quite still.

"Myra," Ralph's voice urged, "did you hear?"

She said through tight lips, "Yes. Yes, I heard," and went to the door and flung it open.

Ralph's eyes appraised her.

"Don't be scared! They want to see you, but it's only

a matter of routine—checking up on everyone in the house. They're good chaps."

"But I wasn't here! Why ask for me?"

"Scotland Yard is very thorough. Now that you're part of the household, you've got to be looked over anyway."

And questioned! *You are Myra Ashlyn? When did you arrive? Your passport, please! My passport!*

"Myra, don't look as though it's the end of the world!" he reached out and touched her arm.

"I'm sorry. But you see, I've never been involved with the police before. And now, having to face them in a strange country—"

"They'll understand. And they'll be kind. Don't worry."

She said a little sickly, "All right. I'll come now."

"That's the girl!" He gave her a bright smile and his hand rested for a moment on her arm.

The police were waiting for her in the drawing room. Old Joss introduced them.

"Inspector Vachell," he said, "and Sergeant Matthews." He turned to the inspector. "My niece has only just arrived from Canada and it's her first visit to England. So be gentle with her."

The inspector smiled.

"Don't worry, sir. We only want to ask her a very few questions. Please sit down, Miss Ashlyn."

Vonnie sat down automatically. She felt dead and heavy as a stone. It was as though fear robbed her of sensation. The door closed behind Old Joss, and she was alone with the police. She heard the inspector ask her if she were Myra Ashlyn.

"Yes," she said, quietly aware, with a kind of impersonal horror, that she had told a lie to the law.

She had come to stay here with her uncle? Yes. Her voice was a whisper. For the life of her she couldn't hide her terror. And how would they interpret it, these quiet, searching men? As guilt? They were asking if this was her first visit to England. Yes, she told them, since she was five years old and her parents had emigrated to

85

Canada. Had she known her Uncle Felix? To the best of her knowledge she had never met him in her life.

And then, with unexpected suddenness it was all over. They had not asked her about her plane flight, had not forced her to detail her time of arrival. But, behind the attitude of calm—ankles crossed, hands folded in her lap—Vonnie knew they were aware of her terror, and she wondered frantically whether the lie about her name was a criminal offense.

"You've had a tragic introduction to England, Miss Ashlyn," the inspector was saying kindly. "I hope the rest of your stay will be happier."

"Thank you."

"That's all for now."

She rose and her knees shook so that she could scarcely reach the door. Sergeant Matthews held the door open for her. Old Joss was sitting in a tall carved chair in the hall. Behind her as she went to him, the inspector called his name.

Joss rose, patted her arm and said "It wasn't too bad, was it?" and disappeared into the drawing room.

The door closed behind him and Vonnie stood for a moment fighting her sense of guilt.

She told herself that no purpose could possibly have been served by telling the inspector the truth. It would only have complicated everything and started a chain of bitterness and recrimination. After all she was a stranger here and there was nothing she could tell that could contribute towards the discovery of a murderer.

Nothing? With a jerk she recalled the light in the attic room. Someone had been in a supposedly empty house and she was the only one who knew. She—and the murderer. . . .

But the British police were notoriously clever at their jobs; they would find the criminal without her slim piece of evidence. And the price for telling was too great, both for old Joss Ashlyn, who had surely suffered sufficient shock already; and for Myra, who had her right to this

86

bid for her happiness. And for me, too, Vonnie thought. *I've plunged into this and I've got to see it through.*

She heard a sound in the dining room and opened the door.

Fenella sat at a table, lighting a cigarette.

"Hello? So they put you through it, too!"

"There was nothing I could tell that would help them."

"No, I suppose not." She pushed the cigarette packet across the table. "Smoke?" With the cigarette at the corner of her mouth, she put up her hands and ran her fingers nervously through her hair. "Why this questioning all over again? We've already been through it heaven knows how many times! And there'll only be the same questions, the same answers—"

"I suppose," Vonnie said, "the inspector thinks someone may recall something he's forgotten; some little thing—"

"I've thought till my brain reels," Fenella said impatiently. "I've offered my suggestion as to what happened, but they won't follow my line of argument. I still believe it was an outsider. Uncle Joss believes the drug was meant for him, but it's ludicrous to think that one of us would want him to come to harm! We're not killers!" she cried. "For heaven's sake, we're civilized people!"

"But someone wasn't," Vonnie said quietly.

"Then it was one of Uncle Felix's enemies—and whatever anyone says, I believe he must have had many. He *was* an outsider! I know Uncle Joss stands up for him, but then I suppose there's a strong feeling of unity between twins and he'd probably stand up for him if it had been Uncle Felix who was the murderer! So, he made enemies and one of them followed him here, saw a grand opportunity—and took a chance on the drug killing him."

"And took a less remote chance that it would be Uncle Joss who drank the brandy!" Vonnie said. "It seems to me that he's right and that someone wanted *him* dead and not Uncle Felix."

The room seemed stifling. She went to the window that looked out onto the high hedge and the road. Two nights ago she had walked past here, had crept near the hedge, around to the back of the garden to look for a magnolia tree and a swing. And someone from a house next door had seen her. And someone, also, had been here, in this supposedly empty house. Someone had switched a light on and off in an attic room. A room that was part of Ralph's flat? Or some storage room? She didn't know yet, but somehow she would have to find out.

"This won't do me any good at the office," Fenella was complaining. "I've got a very conventional boss. You're lucky, being your own boss—"

"Oh, but—" Vonnie began and then stopped sharply.

"But what?"

"But there are compensations," Vonnie said vaguely, covering up for her momentary unthinking.

How easy to make a slip! How frighteningly easy to speak on impulse, forget her role, and ruin everything!

Fenalla said "I know what you mean. Personally I hate responsibility, so a job like yours where you have charge of staff and are responsible for everything you earn would scare me to death. Give me a nice salaried job—or, better still, give me a lot of money and no job at all!" She gave a brief, unamused laugh.

The moment of danger was over. But with each day of familiarity with this family, Vonnie realized she ran the risk of being less and less on her guard. Come to that, how did she know yet that Inspector Vachell had done with her? He might check up on her statements and find that no Myra Ashlyn had taken the flight from Montreal to London that day. . . .

She turned sharply from the window, as though to flee from her haunting thoughts.

"What's the matter?" Fenella stared through the rising coil of cigarette smoke, eyes half closed, watching her.

"The matter?" Vonnie affected surprise, sauntered to the table and took an apple from the silver bowl, "Nothing!"

"Well, I'd never have guessed!" Fenella observed unfriendlily. "I thought at least you'd seen Uncle Felix's ghost outside in the drive the way you leaped away from the window!"

"I wouldn't recognize his ghost if I saw it." Vonnie bit into the apple. "Does Uncle Joss mind us taking fruit?"

"Good heavens, no! There are masses on the shelves in the cellar. He gets a crate sent every year from some orchards in Kent."

Vonnie sat down at the table. The apple was sharp in flavor and hard and its skin had a curious cider smell.

Fenella eyed her.

"You know, I'd advise you to change your mind and go to a hotel. There's no reason on earth why you should remain here. I know Uncle Joss so well; he would understand, and believe me he's not a soft, sentimental old man who'd get hurt. He may seem so to you, but *I* know him!"

"I've come, and I'm staying," Vonnie said with a flash of spirit and tackled her apple.

"I just thought that if you were staying because you felt it would please him and be a kind thing to do, I'd clarify the situation for you, that's all." Fenella leaned over and pulled an ash tray towards her and crushed out her cigarette. "Uncle is tough and he's perfectly self-sufficient. He had a sudden impulse to write to you and ask you over when he was ill because he got in a bit of panic about dying. But he's not going to die, not for a long time, and that, to him, makes the situation very different. A lot of hard men get temporarily soft when they think they're near to dying—maybe it's a bit of old conscience! But they perk up and become themselves again when the crisis is over. Uncle Joss wouldn't mind in the least if you stayed at a hotel. Besides, I'm around—and I understand him. As I told you, we've been very close for years."

"Then I think it's time I became a little close to him too, don't you?" Vonnie said blandly.

Fenella lifted her shoulders.

"Please yourself! I know if *I'd* just come to a house where a murder had been committed and I had the chance to stay in freedom at a hotel, I'd be in the next taxi that crusied past the house!"

It was all too obvious! Fenella didn't want her here. Either the old enmity which as little children had stormed between them was something inherent so far as she was concerned, or she was jealous of her closeness to Uncle Joss. Vonnie saw what Ralph had meant. Fenella needled at things; she couldn't let anything be that annoyed or troubled her. Well, she could stand being needled. She was here and here she would stay for the four promised weeks.

Vonnie finished her apple and went out into the kitchen to throw the core away and wash her hands.

The large almost clinically clean room was empty. Vonnie tossed the core into the bin, rinsed her hands and glanced out of the open back door towards the garden. Someone was standing in the angle between the kitchen wall and the deep bay window of the drawing room, someone pressed well back against the thick glossy green foliage of the magnolia. Someone listening! Vonnie leaned forward and saw that it was Rhoda.

And, as the drawing room windows were open, Rhoda could probably hear most of what was being said between Inspector Vachell and Joss Ashlyn.

She dropped the pink towel back on its roller and went out of the kitchen. Why was Rhoda so interested? Mere curiosity? Or was there some deeper reason for her absorbed interest in what was being said?

Back in the dining room, Fenella had risen and was lighting another cigarette. Four stubs lay in the ashtray.

She's chain smoking, Vonnie thought.

Fenella half turned her head, "All this police questioning!" she exclaimed in a voice breaking with tension. "A ridiculous waste of time—interfering with our lovely lazy afternoon in the garden to ask what's been asked before! Why don't they look outside among Uncle Felix's so-called friends? Or—" she added slowly, "even among Uncle Joss's friends since there's a chance the attempt was on *his* life? It's possible that he lent someone a lot of money and wanted payment and whoever it was, couldn't pay and was desperate and—"

"If that were so, Uncle would surely tell the police!"

Fenella put up her hands and smoothed her raven hair.

"Oh, he does quixotic things. He can be as hard as nails. And he can be almost stupidly understanding. Maybe he likes whoever it was and can't bear to incriminate him."

"I doubt if he'd feel *that* kindly towards him!" Vonnie observed dryly. "Of *course* he'd tell the police if he had any suspicions!"

Fenella said wearily "I was only making suggestions, thinking aloud, if you like. Just trying to make sense of it all!"

Someone was coming down the stairs. Fenella raised her head.

"Ralph?" she called.

There was a pause outside the door.

"Ralph, we're in here!" Fenella's clear voice was carrying and imperious.

The door opened.

Fenella's eyes moved to the raincoat over his arm.

"Where are you going?"

"Out for some air. But there are clouds coming up and there may be thunder, hence the raincoat." He spoke with a forced lightness, edging back towards the hall as though he was in a hurry to get away.

"You'd better stay," Fenella almost snapped. "The police may want to question you, too."

"I have nothing more to tell them!"

"Neither had I, neither had Myra, or Uncle Joss—but they questioned us just the same!" Fenella retorted. "And I don't see why you should try to sneak off—"

"Hey, what's bitten you?"

"A murder investigation," she said shortly. "Your nerves

may be of stronger composition than mine. I hate it—I *loathe* this feeling that the police have the right to walk in here at any moment, question and probe and search our things—as though one of us was the criminal!"

"Well, someone was!"

"Why can't they look around for Uncle Felix's friends?"

"You keep asking that," Ralph protested, tossed his raincoat on a chair and perched on the edge of the table. "It may sound the obvious place for investigation to you, my dear. But it seems it doesn't to the police. They may not have yet decided on Suspect No. 1, but you may be sure it's someone among us."

"You included?"

He grinned at her. "Maybe, me included! Though they'll probably eliminate me pretty quickly. There's no reason on earth why I should want to harm either of your uncles. I'm just an outsider, a lodger."

Fenella looked at him out of eyes that seemed to have changed color, to have become dark and intense.

"*Are* you such an outsider, darling?" she asked softly. "*Are* you so disinterested in my family?"

In the moment's silence, no one moved.

The clock on the mantelpiece was the only sound to be heard. Then Ralph slid from the table.

"Where murder is concerned, Fenella, I'm the complete outsider!" he said equally softly. "Get that quite clear, dear!"

Some strong emotion pulled and tightened between them. Theye were two people who could be lovers—or enemies. And at the moment of watching and listening Vonnie had no way of knowing which it was.

Then Ralph lit a cigarette and the tension snapped.

He said, fidgeting with his lighter. "It's pretty awful to think that if anyone had been in the house at the time your Uncle Felix's life might have been saved. It's one of those tricks of fate, isn't it, that the house was empty that night, otherwise someone would have heard him fall, heard the smash of glass—"

But someone *had* been in the house—someone who had flashed a light on and off in an attic room. Who? Rhoda, now too alarmed at the turn of events, to admit that she had come home early? What was that top back room looking out onto the garden? Part of Ralph's flat? Or a storeroom for all the unwanted and broken bits of furniture, the old mattresses and tennis rackets and heaven knew what, that collected over many years in a house?

Again Vonnie decided that for her own peace of mind she must find out.

There was the sound of a door opening, and of men's voices. Then feet tramped across the parquet flooring and the front door closed.

Ralph craned forward, glancing out of the window. When he spoke, his voice was vibrant with relief.

"They've gone! And for all your dark warnings, Fenella they didn't want to question me!"

"But they'll be back, darling," Fenella said very softly. "Don't be too elated! They'll be back to ask you the same damned questions they asked you before. And woe betide you if you don't give the same answers!"

"I shall! Because I shall be telling the truth."

"You'd better!" she said succinctly. The look she gave him was full of meaning. Of her own brand of sulky love? Or resentment? Or even warning?

VIII

OLD JOSS ENTERED the room. He looked tired and stooped like a great bear, weary after a hunt.

The cat, Prinny, followed him in and when he sat down, jumped on his knees and began to purr.

Vonnie watched the handsome old man. Fenella was right. For all his great size, he had the high color and the restlessness of a heart case. Shock could kill him. Perhaps in the end this tragedy, coming so soon after his illness, would prove fatal. She desperately hoped that he would weather the shocks that might still be in store for him. Because she liked him, because she felt that, whatever his faults, he had irresistible lovableness.

Fenella was asking, "What did the inspector want from you this time, Uncle Joss?"

"To question whether I had ever taken friends into the studio and given them drinks there. I said I hadn't."

"But even if you had, who knew you were allergic to that particular drug?"

He stroked the purring cat on his knees, his hands pressing lightly on the rich black coat.

"When I was thrown into hospital after having taken that sedative, I suppose everyone, more or less, knew about it. I was working at the time on a royal portrait so even the newspapers reported the matter." He looked hunched and old, his great gray head bent over the cat. "I thought I'd lived my life without making enemies. I was mistaken!"

Fenella started up from her chair.

"You haven't enemies!" she swept around the table and

put her arms across the great shoulders in a swift, impulsive gesture. "If anyone really tried to kill you, then— it must have been a madman. Let's go into the drawing room; it's much more comfortable there."

He moved and the cat leaped lightly to the floor.

"I still think, Myra," he said, "I should send you away."

"I won't go!"

"From what I can see of it, this inquiry may last some time."

"But they must stop coming and asking you questions!" Vonnie cried. "There's an end to the things that have to be asked!"

"Not with Inspector Vachell!" Fenella said a little maliciously. "When he comes to the end of the questions he has to ask, he just goes back to the beginning and starts all over again! And so on! And so on! It's a form of third degree—"

Joss said sternly "That's unfair! He's only doing his job, and I should imagine he does it extremely well. He's paid to investigate a murder, and he's going to do just that! Now, let's not discuss it any more. Ralph, join us for dinner, will you?"

"It's kind of you, sir, but I have to go out."

Fenella's head shot up.

"Go out? But you said we shouldn't! You said—"

"I have to go around and see my mother," he cut in, his gaze holding hers a shade defiantly. "My sister rang a little while ago and Mother isn't well."

"Then look in for a nightcap when you get back," Joss suggested.

Ralph said, "Thanks, I'd like to. I won't be late," he looked across the room. "Good-bye, Fenella."

She didn't answer. But when the door had closed behind him, she said with cold fury, "He was going to take me out to a cinema and dinner this evening. And he begged off. Some excuse to the effect that with this tragedy in the house—*his* words, not mine!—it would be better to postpone it. As though we were deeply mourn-

ing someone I loved instead of someone I scarcely knew!
But he can go chasing off to his mother's on some
trumped-up reason!"

"How do you know it's that?" Joss said.

"Because Mrs. Winslow enjoys extremely good health!"

"Even robust people can become ill—"

"I believe it's just an excuse to get out of the house and
away from us!" Fenella blazed. "Since Uncle Felix died,
Ralph has been like a jumpy cat. He gets away from us
as often as he can."

"It's natural, I suppose, that he doesn't want to be involved!"

"Ralph's not the squeamish type! But he has developed
a way of looking over his shoulder—almost as though
there's a ghost around."

"It can't be pleasant living in a house where there's
been a violent death," old Joss said. "Particularly when
you're not even involved with the family, as Ralph certainly isn't."

"That's what *you* think, Uncle Joss!"

Only Vonnie, near Fenella, could have heard her softly
spoken comment.

Joss said, "Let's have drinks. It's after six. Fenella, go
and ask Rhoda what she'd like."

"For heaven's sake, Uncle, she's only the housekeeper!
You don't have to treat her like a—a guest."

"I treat her as she should be treated," old Joss said.
"Rhoda always comes in here for a cocktail before dinner
and you know it quite well. If she's too busy with the
meal to come, perhaps you or Myra would take one out
to her."

Vonnie rose.

"I'll go and ask her, Uncle Joss."

No one protested.

Rhoda, in a white coat over her dress, was coping with
minute steaks. All the necessary garnishings were laid
out neatly on the enameled top of a little table near the
stove—mushrooms and tomatoes and watercress. She

looked up as Vonnie entered and smiled. She had a slow, grave smile that barely touched her eyes, and her carriage, as she stood at the stove, was one of pride. She did her job superbly, accepted her salary, but there was not a trace of servility about her. She was an equal, and her poise and her carriage were those of a hostess graciously preparing a meal for her guests.

She said, "Ah, Miss Ashlyn. I do hope you have everything you need. Is your room comfortable?"

"It's charming. Did you arrange the flowers?"

"Yes. I do them all through the house."

"They're so beautifully done."

Rhoda smiled and wiped the small, brilliantly red tomatoes.

"Oh, I took a course in flower arrangement. It's just one of the many things I've done in my life."

"Uncle Joss sent me to ask if you're joining us for drinks."

Rhoda shook her head. Her bare forearms below the short white sleeves of her overall were as rounded as those of a young girl.

"I can't leave the cooking," she said. "But thank him. I'll have a martini out here."

Again, Vonnie thought, accepting the offer of a drink brought to her as though it were her right.

"Did I hear Ralph go out?"

"Yes. He has gone to see his mother."

Rhoda made a gesture of annoyance.

"He hasn't a refrigerator and he always comes down to us if he wants ice. He's taken some up to his flat in the waterjug your uncle particularly likes to have in the dining room! Miss Ashlyn, I can't leave my cooking. Do you think you could go up and fetch it for me, please?"

"But can I get into his flat?"

"It isn't self-contained. It's the three rooms on the top floor. Just climb the stairs and you'll probably find the doors wide open. You don't mind going?"

"Of course not, providing Ralph won't object to my going into his rooms?"

"Oh, he comes down here when he likes. It's a free-and-easy arrangement between your uncle and him. A little too free—" She stopped abruptly, her voice brisk again. "Thank you, if you would fetch the jug." Then she smiled. "Like all cooks at this time of evening, my hands are rather full!"

On the top floor, as Rhoda had said, the doors were wide open. The first was a room little bigger than a large cupboard fitted up as a kitchen. The waterjug wasn't in there, but melting ice cubes were ranged in a bowl around a bottle of bitter lemon. The other open door led to the sitting room.

Vonnie went in. It was a long low room with one small sash window; pleasant enough, but entirely without personality. The chairs were dark leather, old and very much used; the carpet was a deep red and blue with an ugly geometrical design. Bookshelves lined two walls and there were no flowers. A television stood on a low table and on the wall were half a dozen photographs of college groups. It was a totally inartistic room, obviously furnished by pieces from Ralph's old home. Vonnie saw the glass jug on a table by the window.

And then as she picked it up she realized that she was in the room where she had seen the light flick on and off two nights ago.

This must mean that Ralph had been in the house at the time of Felix Ashlyn's death. She glanced down and saw the studio below jutting out to her left.

It was a quiet road, with little traffic, and here, at the back, were the gardens and the trees and nothing to drown the sound of a heavy fall and shattered glass. So that whoever was here must have heard.

But Ralph had said he was out.

Or had he been speaking the truth? His flat was not self-contained, so anyone could have entered the room, just as she was entering it now. Who then had flicked the light on in this room? Rhoda? Even old Joss himself? But that was absurd. Old Joss Ashlyn would never kill his own brother!

But at the dawn of civilization, Cain had killed Abel. It had been the first reported murder in the history of the world. Men killed their brothers! But not Joss. Not that splendid, likable old man . . . All the same, how did she know whether he was capable of murder or not? What did she know of any of them? She wasn't even of their blood! She was a stranger in a world of ease and comfort —and violent death. . . .

Yet she saw how easy it would be to become immersed in the mystery in this house, and how dangerous that could be for her. It would place her off her guard with her own position here. She must concern herself only very superficially with the Ashlyn tragedy. To watch herself in case by a single word she gave herself away—that was surely enough for her to cope with . . . !

Still, as she carried the heavy cut glass jug back to the kitchen, the insistent question was there, snaking in her mind. Was the killer of Felix Ashlyn one of these with whom she talked and laughed and ate?

She threw out this impotent questioning and entering the kitchen, said to Rhoda:

"Shall I fill the jug and take it into the dining room on my way?"

"Thank you, if you would."

"And—" Vonnie began a little shyly. "I'd like it if you'd call me Myra."

"Of course," Rhoda said politely. "Your uncle has a dislike for surnames—it could be called an artist's idiosyncrasy!" her lips curved in amusement, "so Christian names are the order of the day here."

Or, Vonnie thought remembering Fenella's malicious little comments, it could be because Rhoda had in the past always been "Rhoda" to Joss Ashlyn and she had no intention of being treated as anything but an equal either by him or his family! But that was their affair.

In the drawing room, Fenella looked up from the corner of the settee where she sat, slender legs crossed, a white bolero over her sun dress.

"Have you been getting to know our Rhoda?"

"In a way, yes."

"Is she joining us?" old Joss asked.

"No, but she'd like a martini. I'll take it out to her, but I'm afraid I don't know how to mix one."

Fenella got up lazily.

"I'll do it! I could," she gave a curious little muffled giggle, "give her nine-tenths gin and a drop of martini and see whether her dignity becomes ruffled."

"Fenella!"

"Well, Uncle Joss, if you like your housekeeper to behave like a *grande dame*, that's fine. But personally I'd like to see how she behaves under the influence of drink. That's when people show their real selves!"

"I wouldn't," Vonnie said. "I'd just go to sleep. They always welcome me at cocktail parties in Vancouver because all I ever have is one drink. Two, and my eyes begin to close!"

"Just as well," Uncle Joss said, "I dislike women who boast of the amount they can take. That's one thing about our family, we have our drink before lunch and before dinner. Apart from that, I'm the only old sinner who likes a whisky during the evening. But then, at my age, I can indulge."

"I'll take Rhoda's martini to her," Fenella said, and carried it with a steady hand out of the room.

"I'm afraid your first day here hasn't been pleasant," Joss said. "Particularly the police visit. But I had to tell them of your visit."

"Of course you did, Uncle Joss, and it's perfectly all right."

"Perhaps when we get over the next few days the case will be cleared up and we can live our normal lives again. Until it is, I'm afraid there won't be much gadding, for me at any rate. Have you friends in town who could take you around? If so, do contact them. Get out as much as you can—after all, there's no reason for you to sit cooped up here."

"Oh, I'll get around."

"*Have* you friends here?" he asked again.

Vonnie shook her head.

"I seem to remember," he said slowly, "some people called Garvin. Mary Garvin was a school friend of your mother's and I believe they kept up a regular correspondence with each other until your mother died. There was a son and a daughter, wasn't there? And they had a house in Chelsea. Now if we looked them up in the telephone directory—"

"Please don't bother, Uncle Joss," Vonnie said quickly —too quickly! "Let me just wander around and get the 'feel' of London on my own."

"But if you met the Garvins they could take you around and introduce you to other people."

"We'll see later. Please—" she urged as the old man turned towards the telephone directories on a shelf, "I'd rather you didn't bother just yet!"

He looked nonplussed.

"Very well, but surely you kept in touch with them!"

A girl and boy of Myra's age? The name rang a faint bell. Had Myra told her that Marian Garvin was married? Or had it been someone else? She thought, with a small panic, I mustn't meet them! Myra probably sent them a snap of herself some time or other, or told them something in a letter that I know nothing about. . . .

Old Joss was watching her with a faintly puzzled look.

"You didn't write to them that you were coming over?"

"No."

"But whenever people visit another country, they always take care to let the friends they have there know. Now if you—"

"Please Uncle Joss," Vonnie interrupted with a small rising panic, "I'd so much rather get around on my own, at any rate to begin with!"

Joss gave her a doubtful, indulgent smile.

"If you'd really like it that way and aren't just being shy—"

"I'm not being shy," Vonnie said with feeling.

Suddenly, sharply, the telephone bell rang.

Joss went into the hall to answer it, leaving the door ajar.

Vonnie sat quietly and flagrantly listened.

"Yes. Yes, speaking. Oh? Well, what is it you have to tell me." There was a listening pause. Then, "You are sure it was a woman? In a dark suit? Yes. Yes. No, don't come and tell me about it. Get in touch with the police. They're the people who should know. Ask for Inspector Vachell. Yes, that's the name. At Scotland Yard. Right! Good-bye."

Vonnie was staring towards the door as old Joss returned. He sat down heavily in his chair.

"That was a woman who has been staying with some friends in the house you see between those trees at the end of the garden. She left yesterday morning for her home in the country. She now rings up to say that as she was packing two nights ago, she looked out of the window and she saw a woman in our garden. She says she seemed to be hovering. It was too dark to see her face, but she wore a dark-colored suit. I've told her to report it to the police. But it does bear out the maid Greta's report, doesn't it? She, too, saw a woman in the garden here."

Vonnie felt herself crouching back into the soft cushions of the settee. A woman in the garden at the time of the murder . . . a woman in a dark suit . . . a dark suit? *That's right. It's blue . . . and it's mine!*

IX

VONNIE SLEPT badly that night. There was too much on her mind, too many disturbing elements, developments that could involve her.

She went to bed at eleven, but at half past twelve the house still did not sleep. In Rhoda's room, next to hers, she heard movement and, as the clock struck midnight, Rhoda went quietly downstairs again. Vonnie did not explain, even to herself, the lurking suspicion that made her get out of bed and go to the window. But she did just that and saw that a light was on in the studio.

Why had Rhoda chosen a time when everyone was safely in their rooms to prowl around there? What was she looking for? Most certainly it was not a room in which she could have left something of her own—the novel she was reading or her cigarette case. From her window Vonnie could not see her but she had gone back to bed and had lain for a long time listening before she heard Rhoda return.

Vonnie tossed off a blanket and was immediately cold. She pulled it back again and lay on her side. Her gaze moved for a moment to the wall and saw, in the faint light of the moon, the blurred outline of the painting on the wall.

Quickly she shut her eyes but the image was there. The sea and the radiant sunset—and with it the memory of Nigel . . . The puzzle and ache of that betrayal of love was still with her an hour later when she drifted into sleep.

The daily newspapers still ran up-to-the-minute reports of the Ashlyn tragedy. Vonnie sitting in the garden the following morning, reading the Sunday news, saw that a notice of her visit to the house in St. John's Wood had been released to the press: "Myra Ashlyn, a niece from Canada!"

It was another hot day and Fenella had come around, armed again with books and writing pad to spend the morning in the garden.

Her flat, she explained, was on the second floor of a tall block and was hot and stuffy in hot weather.

"And anyway," she added, "this is a time when I feel we should rally around Uncle as much as possible. At least—" she added, meaningly. "*I* should. *You* don't have to stay around."

"Thanks, but I'm quite happy!" Vonnie said firmly. Then, because she had to talk about it, "I'm mentioned this morning in the newspaper."

Fenella gave a brief laugh, flung herself down in a garden chair and raised her arms to the sun.

"Well, why worry? You're a nice bit of romance to color the tragedy! 'Joss Ashlyn's niece walks into tragedy.' 'Beautiful young girl from our commonwealth stays with famous artist uncle.' That sort of thing! And the public will love it; it'll renew their interest in the murder hunt. That's the trouble! People get so easily bored with news—they've got to have a fresh angle, a new snippet, something to whet their satiated appetites! Don't worry!" She stretched her fingers, looking at them as her nails gleamed deep pink in the sunlight. "The next thing will be they'll be around here for a photograph of you."

Fresh alarm struck Vonnie like a blow.

"Oh no, *not that*!" The paper dropped from her hands. She stared around at Fenella in dismay. "They mustn't!"

"Who mustn't do what?" old Joss asked from behind them.

He came and sat down in the **big** wicker chair that was kept especially for him, settled himself, and said "Hello, Fenella, my dear. Nice to see you around so early!"

"It was such a hot night I couldn't sleep. So I got up at eight this morning and I thought of your garden. You don't mind me crashing in like this, do you?"

"My dear child, I've told you a dozen times, come around when you want to. I like to have my own around me—and how anyone can live without a garden in the summer, I don't know."

"Some have to," Fenella said bitterly, "since land in London is too valuable to give us all gardens!"

"By the way, what were you so upset about?" he asked Vonnie.

She tapped the newspaper on her lap.

"I'm mentioned here and Fenella says the reporters may come around for a photograph of me. And they mustn't!"

"Well, we'll tell them so," he said easily. "We'll say you're not concerned with all this and you must be left out of their news."

"Though," Fenella said conjecturingly, "I don't know why you have to get so fussed up about it. Most people like to see their pictures in the papers."

"But I don't!" Vonnie burst out.

She sat back, body tense. She had a sudden terrified feeling that at any moment a news photographer might slip around the side of the house and catch her unawares as she sat there in the garden. She got up and moved her chair so that her back was towards the path that ran around the side of the house.

"Too much sun?" Joss inquired.

She said vaguely that it was, that she didn't like it in her eyes.

"But haven't you any sunglasses?"

She had, of course, somewhere still in her suitcase. She hadn't thought of them. The light was actually not nearly so strong as she was used to in summer back there on the Pacific coast, so that she had not bothered to get them out. Now she saw that it could be the solution if any photographer popped in front of her with a camera.

She went into the house and fetched them. They were large and white-framed and they hid her eyes completely.

Down in the garden again, Joss said with kindly reassurance, "Don't worry about the Press, my dear. I'm sure they'll leave you out of all this. If they become troublesome, just refer them to me. But I don't think they will. They're decent chaps. They just try hard because news is the thing by which they earn their living."

"I've never before known anyone to be squeamish about having his photograph in the papers. Unless he's a recluse, and you aren't one!" There was a narrowed curiosity on Fenella's face. "Don't you ever have your photograph taken?"

"Occasionally, by friends. It's the idea of publicity that I hate."

"Myra has a right to her feelings in this matter," Joss said. "Where's my newspaper?"

Vonnie said shakenly, "Here," and gathered up the sheets of the one on her lap.

He looked at it, and flung it onto the grass.

"That's not mine! Ah, here it is. That one you've been reading is a rag I order every week for Little Woody. She comes every day except Saturdays—Sundays only for an hour—and she loves to take that paper home and wallow in it!"

"Then I'd better take it in to her."

"No, leave it. She won't want it till she goes home at half past eleven."

"I told you," Fenella said impatiently. "Rhoda mustn't do rough work! That's what our Little Woody does—all the scrubbing and the sweeping and the polishing. She's only nineteen but her hands are red and her nails are broken and I've never seen her in anything but shoes scuffed at the toes with all the kneeling she does."

"She doesn't have to kneel," old Joss said. "We keep mops and a Hoover. What she does here is about the limit of her capabilities. She'd be useless in an office or a shop. And she likes it. Funny, you sometimes find these mentally retarded people excellent with good honest housework," he rustled his newspaper. "What are you going to do today? I'd like to have taken you somewhere —to the Zoo or Kew Gardens. But I think I'd better stay in."

"And anyway, Uncle, the crowds will be terrific everywhere today and it's so hot!" Fenella leaned back and closed her eyes. "Please Myra, don't ask me to take you and show you the sights—not today!"

"I won't. I promise!" Vonnie assured her easily. "Perhaps later I'll go for a walk and get my bearing."

"Regent's Park is just opposite. And if you like to take a bus down the road you can get to Marble Arch and listen to the soapbox orators. They're quite amusing the first time. After that, you avoid that bit of Hyde Park like the plague."

Vonnie knew perfectly well that Fenella was doing all she could to brush aside any suggestion that she should take old Joss's visitor around. She hadn't invited her and she hadn't the slightest intention of putting herself out for her. It was, in fact, strange that someone as beautiful as Fenella should have no one calling to take her into the country or to the sea on such a day. But then Fenella was probably only here at all because Ralph lived upstairs; these frequent visits were possibly to stake—and keep—her claim on him.

Was it a mutual love? Or was it one-sided? Was it love at all? Could this constant appearance at the house have to do with Felix Ashlyn's death, because Fenella was suspicious and was watching someone? Did she sit here, facing the house, seemingly drowsing in the sun, in order to observe the house and those who lived in it . . . ?

Vonnie looked at her. She appeared to have her eyes closed but Vonnie saw the gleam of vivid blue slits and knew that, beneath those white lids, Fenella was alert and watching.

At twelve o'clock, she and Ralph had a date for drinks with some friends. Old Joss, watching Fenella walk into the house on her way to her flat to change into a dress, turned to Vonnie.

"They should take you along with them!"

"But I don't want to go," she said honestly. "I'd much rather go for a walk on my own."

He looked at her doubtfully.

"I really mean that! I don't want to spend the next hour drinking someone's cocktails, especially on such a lovely morning," she laughed. "I'm much more the fresh air type. I'd rather like to go for a walk now, if you wouldn't mind."

"Come and go as you like," he urged.

On her way into the house, Vonnie had to pass the small room with the picture window, known as the garden room because it contained deck chairs, heaps of bright cushions and a few plants in pots.

Ralph was there and greeted her. "You were up early this morning! I saw you from my window. I'm lazy on a Sunday. I lie in bed, drink coffee and read the papers." His eyes went over her head and she turned to see what was interesting him.

From where they stood they could look, at an angle, into the studio. The great windows gaped, gleaming in the sunlight and standing in the room; looking at a tall panel of broken glass which seemed to be held upright by some iron vises was Rhoda.

"That," Ralph said, "is the panel against which your Uncle Felix fell. It was nearly finished and a lovely piece of work, all brilliant greens and violets and crimsons, representing the life of St. Andrew."

Vonnie could see the great gaps in the design where the light shone through the smashed glass. Rhoda was wandering about the room. She had a cigarette between her fingers and she seemed to be not so much looking for something as deep in thought. And Vonnie remembered how last night Rhoda had gone secretly to the studio!

"I wonder what Rhoda is doing in there," Ralph said thoughtfully.

"She has probably been dusting—"

"With a cigarette in her fingers and no duster? No, I think she's there because it's the scene of the murder. Some people have morbid minds, you know!"

But not Rhoda, Vonnie thought. She was too civilized, too intelligent. There was some other reason for her quiet visits to the studio. She might even be sleuthing on her own, looking for a clue the police had missed.

"I'm hanging around," Ralph was saying, "waiting for Fenella. We're going to some friends for drinks—" He hesitated and looked at her doubtfully. "I wish we could ask you to come with us. Only they're more Fenella's friends than mine."

"Thank you, but I wouldn't come anyway. I thought of going out for a walk."

"On your own! For Pete's sake, this is a fine way for us to be treating a visitor!"

"But the circumstances aren't exactly normal, are they?" Vonnie said gently. "Nothing can be planned for anyone at the moment. I see that. I was prepared for it when I decided not to go to a hotel, as Uncle Joss suggested, but to stay here. I'm not pining for parties. I came to see Uncle Joss and I can enjoy myself perfectly well wandering around London on my own."

"Nevertheless," Ralph said softly. "I wish you were coming with us! You know, if you're typical of Canadian girls, I think I'll emigrate."

"That's a nice compliment, Ralph, thank you!"

They both laughed and as Vonnie turned, she saw that Rhoda was no longer in the studio. Silently, she had gone. And nobody, perhaps, would ever know her feelings as she had stood alone by the shattered stained glass panel. . . .

Late that afternoon, Vonnie explored the garden room. She found in it a croquet set, playing cards, a chess set and the paraphernalia for an old man's recreation. There was also a gramophone and a pile of old records.

Vonnie was looking through them when she heard in the distance the telephone bell ringing. Footsteps hurried along the hall to the alcove where the telephone stood. Then Rhoda came back down the passage towards the sun room, calling Myra's name.

"There's someone asking for you," she said.

Vonnie said, startled, "But Rhoda, it could be a reporter! And I don't want to speak to him."

"I don't think it is. You'd better go, anyway. If you find it's someone you don't want to talk to, you can easily hang up."

Someone she didn't want to talk to? She wanted to talk to no one! But Rhoda was standing there, slender, neat, poised in brown linen and brown and white shoes.

"It's probably some friend of yours who has learned that you're in England."

Some friend of Myra's! Vonnie said, weakly, "Yes, perhaps that's it. Thank you, Rhoda," and went down the hall to the telephone alcove.

With a thudding heart she lifted the receiver. Before she actually spoke, she took a grip on herself. Nobody could see her. The telephone was just a tube down which her voice went. She was invisible to whoever waited to speak to her; safe so long as she was cautious and kept her head. She took a deep breath. Then, in a low voice as near Myra's husky tones as she could manage, she said, "Myra Ashlyn speaking."

"Myra! This is Nigel Foster."

The hall spun dizzily around her. She reached back with a foot groping for a chair, dragged it toward her, and sank into it. Her heart was hammering so much that it seemed to shake her whole body: her hand felt clammy on the receiver.

"Hello—Myra?" came Nigel's impatient voice. "Are you still there?"

"Yes," she said faintly.

"Yours is a dreadful introduction to London," he said soberly, "and I hope, for your sake, the whole affair will be cleared up quickly."

"Thank you," Vonnie said weakly, and waited.

"It was a struggle to ring you in the circumstances but I had to. Myra, I won't keep you talking, but please tell me—"

"Tell you—what?"

"I've got to find Vonnie! Where is she?"

The receiver was clutched so tightly that her hand ached. On her right the door to the living room was ajar, and in there someone could be listening to this staccato, one-sided conversation. Uncle Joss . . .

"I tried three times to get through to her in Vancouver," Nigel was explaining. "But there was no reply from your flat. I've also written to Vonnie and had no answer."

"I can explain—"

Her voice must have been too faint for him to hear for he cut in, demanding, "What has happened to her? To both of you? Where is Vonnie?"

(*Here, Nigel darling, here! Talking to you, careful to disguise her voice because people—strangers—mustn't know the truth!*)

"Are you still there?" his voice rose, demanding.

"Yes."

"Myra, I'm sorry! I know it's a bad time to ring you up, but somehow I've got to get in touch with Vonnie."

"She was in Vancouver for a long time after you left for Yellowknife. You could have got in touch with her then—" There was edge and bitterness in her voice.

"I've an explanation for that! One I have first of all to give Vonnie."

"How did you find me?"

It was an unnecessary question, asked in order to

cover up her shaken half-conviction that this was all a dream.

"Finding you was easy," Nigel said. "I read the newspaper account of your uncle's death." His voice held slight impatience at her questioning and dissembling. "I know you don't want to be bothered with people outside the family at a time like this. So, if you'll just tell me where I can get in touch with Vonnie—"

"Write to her," she said quickly. "Nigel, write to Vonnie at this address."

"You mean, she's there with you?" His voice was charged with such sudden, wild hope that Vonnie nearly broke down and told him. "Myra—" he rushed on, his voice light and boyish with hope, "you mean, she's actually here—in England?"

"Yes. No. *No!* But I'll see she gets the letter."

"Why did you say 'Yes' first and then deny it?" His mood changed swift as lightning. He was angry and impatient again. "I'm sorry, but this is serious for me! Is Vonnie there, or isn't she?"

"I—Nigel, if you'll send a letter to this address—" she began.

"I've not the slightest intention of writing to her care of you!" His voice was clear and hard. "I want Vonnie's address."

"But I promise you faithfully if you'll only send a letter here—"

"Would you care to tell me why you're being so secretive?" his voice was now dangerously quiet, so quiet that she had to strain to hear. "What's happened that I mustn't contact Vonnie direct? For Pete's sake, perhaps you don't know! She and I are—were—in love. Maybe she's changed her mind, but I've got to know that for myself."

"You went away, didn't you? You left her—"

"That's something I've got to talk out with her! *Where is she?*"

"I can't give you her address. I'm sorry, Nigel. You

must believe me when I say, I just can't! I—I would if I could. But if you'll write a letter—" She paused, heard a faint click and cried desperately. "Nigel? Hello—*Hello!*"

But it was as she feared. The line was dead. He had hung up on her.

Vonnie laid the receiver on its cradle and sat staring at the wall. For a moment she had to stop and think where she was. Nigel's voice had dissolved the present.

She crouched with her hands tensed in her lap, stunned by a second shock in two days. Nigel had called her and she hadn't dared to admit that hers was the low, cautious voice which had, through all the shock and wonder and despair of hearing his voice, managed miraculously to keep its husky Myra Ashlyn pitch.

If Nigel had telephoned her in Vancouver and had written to her, then he must have done all this after the apartment was closed. His letters would be lying there in the square postbox because she hadn't dared ask for anything to be sent on. But all this must have happened within the last week. With one of those twists and mockeries of fortune, Nigel must have tried to come back into her life at the very time when she had given up her own identity. . . .

Movement in the living room behind her jerked her back to her own danger. With the door ajar, old Joss must have overheard a lot that had been said. He would be interested, curious as to the meaning of that desperate one-sided conversation he had overheard. And Vonnie couldn't face more lies for the moment.

She rose swiftly, rushed towards the stairs and took them two at a time. Closing the door of her bedroom, she leaned against it, trying to shake herself out of shock.

What explanation could Nigel give for that silence? It could be, she supposed, that there had been some obstacle to their love which he had not had the courage to tell her about. A fiancée in England? A wife, even? The thought was ugly and unpalatable but men did these things. For some reason, if they were holidaying alone, there were those who could not resist playing a bachelor role. But not Nigel! Surely she knew him better than to believe he had lied his way into her heart! Or did you know people? After all, she would have defended him against anyone who had foretold that he would "kiss and ride away"! Yet that was exactly what he had done!

Again, suppose there had been a divorce pending, that it had now been made absolute and he was free? Suppose he hadn't dared tell her because he was not certain of her reaction! Love, she thought, was often so finely balanced that people were afraid to speak, to tell facts as they were. They trusted to luck, to the future, to solve whatever problem there was. . . . Had Nigel done that?

But he should have known her well enough to make the circumstances clear; trust was important in love. . . .

Suddenly, violently, she pushed herself away from the door and crossed to the window looking down on the half blazing, half shadowed garden.

Who was she to talk of trust? Had she trusted him on the telephone just now? Had *she* told him the truth and let him judge her?

She knew now what she should have done. If she had thought quickly enough she would have asked Nigel to meet her somewhere away from the house. Then she would have confronted him with the truth and trusted him to understand. After all, he would have an explanation for her and expect her to understand!

It would have been a mutual test. But she had needed too much time to gather her shaken wits, and Nigel had been impatient. Dismay occupied her immediate thoughts, but deeper down, like the background music for a drama, was the realization that Nigel was in London. His voice had sounded so near that he could have been telephoning from around the corner. But for all she knew where he lived, he might have been five or fifty miles away. She knew that he had given up his flat and stored his furniture when he was sent to Canada. He had told her this first when they were in the train and again as they were sitting on the quayside on Vancouver Island, watching a ship edge into the dock.

"When I get back, I'll stay in a hotel till I can look around and find something."

She remembered now, with a twist of pain, her unshadowed happiness at the time. The sun had been warm on her back and Nigel's hand had been touching hers. Beyond the quay, the Pacific glittered like a golden carpet stretched from Vancouver to Japan.

"Funny thing, Vonnie," Nigel had said, "how so many people want to get out of London, to find a little place in the country and commute. I don't. I love the city. I like to hear the distant roar of the traffic; I like looking out of my window onto a London Square; I like the red buses and the people, new buildings and old. It's a conglomeration, but it's typically London, growing up higgledy-piggledy through generations."

And from somewhere in this vast city he had telephoned her and she had denied herself!

From the mantelpiece an antique carriage clock mocked her with its soft ticking; outside, the sun gilded the tops of the trees and the black cat prowled in the bushes.

Vonnie turned away and stood in front of the dressing table mirror. She picked up a hairbrush and ran it hard through her hair so that her scalp tingled. Then she put on fresh lipstick and powdered her hot forehead.

But she felt no better. She washed her hands at the pale green basin, dried them slowly, looking around the charming room that was a reminder of the crazy thing she had done so honestly and impetuously from her heart.

For Myra, she thought, there had been a solution. She had had her second chance and had seized it like any sensible person.

If only, Vonnie thought, she had kept her head, grasped her chance, too! Asked Nigel to meet her somewhere and told him the truth. But when emotions seized hold of you, clear thinking was impossible. And now, how to find him among the eight million people of London? How to find him when she had forgotten the name of the firm for whom he worked in London. Surely she should have remembered that, could even do so if she tried! But she knew that when he had told her, it had been a vague name in a country six thousand miles away. . . . It had not mattered. Nothing had mattered save their love and their being together. Vaguely at the back of her mind she had believed that she would, in the future, know the name of that firm all too well—know it because that was where her husband worked. And in the meantime there was love to be known and savored. Practical things could wait!

She had a violent desire to get out of the house. To free herself, not only from the oppression of its tragedy but also from the things that would mock at her. The chair in the alcove on which she had sunk when she heard Nigel's voice, the white telephone, the hall itself, dissolving into the dark reality of what she had lost because she had not been able to think quickly or clearly enough.

She kicked off her sandals, found a pair of tennis court shoes, flung a light linen coat over her shoulders and went downstairs.

Old Joss was poring over a book on medieval stained glass. He looked up and smiled at her, insisting that she must feel free to come and go as she liked. He would like to have had a stroll himself, but he had better be on hand in case Inspector Vachell called again. And anyway, his slow pace would be dull for her.

"Next week," he said, "we'll start getting you around a bit. I'll talk to friends of mine who have young people for you to meet. But for the moment, I can do nothing."

She said gently, "Let's leave meeting people, Uncle Joss. I'm a very self-contained person. I've told you, I'll enjoy going around on my own."

"At your age, Myra, you should have an escort!"

Her laughter was a little forced.

"Maybe I'll find one before my stay is over!" she said lightly and meaninglessly.

"And talking of young men," he continued, "I haven't yet discovered the setup between Ralph and Fenella! You're a stranger among us and strangers sometimes see more. What do you think? Are they in love?"

"If they were, surely they'd tell you!" she said evasively.

"I don't know," he seemed puzzled and a little distressed. "Sometimes I think they're in love and holding back. Sometimes I think they're almost enemies. I can't make them out, either of them. There's a strange atmosphere in this house, Myra, and it doesn't seem to me to be entirely due to Felix's murder! There's a kind of tension between them all—Fenella and Ralph—and Rhoda. But I suppose that's their affair. I'm too old to be troubled by other people's animosities. Perhaps when this murder is cleared up the other tensions will disappear. You know—" he gave her a sudden almost impish grin, "there's a lot to be said for being a bachelor! At least whatever private fights go on in this house, I'm free of responsibility. Thank God I've no wife or children to have to battle for and defend!" His shoulders heaved as he chuckled.

It was the first time Vonnie had glimpsed the innate self-absorption that had years ago enabled him to wash the little emigrating Ashlyn family out of his mind.

Myra had once said, "Uncle Joss is so strong. He doesn't need family ties or family affection."

But Vonnie wondered, as she went down the drive and into the street, whether it was strength to stand alone or weakness that dreaded responsibility—and suspected the latter.

She found herself in a matter of minutes in Regent's Park. Walking, however, did not ease her pain of knowing that, through shock, she had handled things badly.

117

She watched the people, the children by the lake, the couples, and felt for the first time a sense of great loneliness. Everyone had someone for a companion, even if it were only a dog. She walked alone, head up, wind blowing softly through her hair, and no one smiled at her, and no one spoke. No one belonged!

Somewhere ahead of her she saw a man with a camera. Immediately she was alerted. She turned quickly. He might, of course, be just someone taking pictures of the park. But on the other hand, he could be a news photographer who had followed her from the house. She was too ignorant of the ways of the Press, the type of cameras they used, to know for certain. But she had to be prepared all the time for the unexpected, the moment of danger; and she did not dare risk her photograph appearing in the newspapers.

She dug her hands in the big patch pockets of her linen coat and her fingers closed on her sunglasses. She must have slipped them in without realizing it. Thankfully she put them on and felt as though the big lenses and the heavy frames were a certain disguise.

Presently she went home. Crossing the road she saw buses pass, advertising theaters. She must go to some, spend her days and her evenings in activity. She made a note of the titles of two plays she saw advertised and decided to ask Fenella which of them was worth a visit.

Fenella! Had there been no tragedy in the house, would Fenella have taken her around a little and introduced her to people? She doubted it. The attitude of Myra's cousin seemed to state very clearly, "Uncle Joss invited you over. It's up to him to look after you. Don't expect me to put myself out!"

Well, thought Vonnie honestly, fair enough. Fenella had her own life, her own friends. She and Myra had neither corresponded nor ever, it seemed, shown liking for each other. Why should she be expected to entertain her merely because there was a supposed family link between them?

118

Rhoda was sitting with old Joss when Vonnie returned. As she entered the drawing room she had a feeling of a conversation snapped off suddenly at her approach.

Joss said, "Sergeant Matthews called soon after you left. He has taken away the frame for the church panel I was doing. He didn't tell me why, but I doubt if it's for fingerprints. That job was done when I first called the police."

Rhoda was sitting back in her chair, her eyes veiled by dark lashes, her hands folded with a display of quietude which Vonnie doubted was genuine.

"And by the way," Joss went on, "I was asked if Felix had ever been in Canada."

"And had he?"

"He may have been. He never could stay in one place, nor could he make good anywhere."

Vonnie sat down heavily in a chair, "You mean, Uncle Joss, that they're now wondering if I—I knew him out here?"

"Oh, I shouldn't think so!" he said easily—too easily, Vonnie thought.

"But I *didn't* know him. And even if I did, why should come all the way over here and harm him?"

Rhoda made her first sign of animation. Her white ids lifted.

"But you *weren't* here when Felix was killed, were ou?"

Vonnie held her breath, steadying herself, and realized once more how, off her guard, she had nearly given herself away, nearly admitted obliquely that she was in London at the time of his death!

"Questions about Felix's movements," old Joss said, are pure outside chances! The fact still remains that the olice believe the drink was meant for me. But they ever pursue one track. Their minds work every way, n the assumption, I suppose, that some small thing in ne branch of inquiry will lead to a solution in another. think murder investigation is rather like a tree. They start at the top, work down along all the myriad branches and then come finally to the root of the thing."

Rhoda said with slow, quiet violence, "I never wanted Felix here, Joss! You knew that I had a strong feeling that he'd bring trouble!"

He looked across at her, smiling with raised eyebrows. "You were in fact psychic at that moment, weren't you?"

She said gravely, "I was."

Psychic? Or had she known Felix in the past and did she bear him an old grudge?

Rhoda glanced at the clock and stirred, "I'd better start dinner. Fenella won't be coming tonight. She told me she and Ralph were having dinner out somewhere."

"She's going to look in later," the old man smiled. "It's unusual to have such attention in the young! But Fenella really does watch over me!"

Rhoda said, "Yes, she does, doesn't she?" but her words had no warmth and her lips curled into what might have been a smile or a tiny sneer.

The clock was striking nine when Fenella returned with Ralph. They brought with them three long-playing records.

Fenella was in silver gray linen with a bunchy, shaggy, shocking pink bolero.

"We're going upstairs to try these on Ralph's gramophone. I suppose—" she looked at her uncle, at Vonnie, at Rhoda last of all. "I suppose there've been no developments."

"Only one," Joss said and told her that the panel had been taken away.

She stood quite quietly. Then she turned to Ralph.

"Go on up to your flat. I'll follow."

She waited until the door was closed and then demanded, "What on earth did they want the panel for?"

"I don't know. I'm not a policeman," he said. "But don't worry!"

"That's just what I *am* doing! Suppose the attempt was really on your life and not on Uncle Felix's? And suppose the murderer tries again? The police haven't taken that panel just out of interest, to see how you work in stained glass. They've got some new idea—a development. Uncle, don't you see? That means whoever killed Uncle Felix must be getting doubly scared, and perhaps desperate."

"So much the better," old Joss said. "Then he'll get careless."

"Or he may try—to—to harm you so as to make it seem that you—you were conscience-stricken."

"You really think," he demanded, "that someone is going to be so desperate that he'll kill me and make it seem that I committed suicide because I was the murderer and couldn't live with my remorse? Really, Fenella, you have a most fertile imagination!"

"All right, you can laugh at me, but you will be careful, won't you?"

"Short of employing a drink-taster like the Medicis in medieval times, I don't quite see what I can do!"

"They won't try *that* again. Next time it could be—oh, it could be anything. Something in your food—"

"My dear Fenella," Rhoda said in her quiet, cool voice. "If any food is tampered with here, then *I* shall be suspect Number 1, shan't I?"

The eyes of the two women met.

"Now look," Joss said quickly, "We're beginning to talk nonsense! Let's drop the subject."

The doorbell rang as he finished speaking. Rhoda rose as Fenella cried, "Oh no, the police again! Uncle, if it is, do you think they're suspecting one of us and are trying to break down our resistance?"

"My dear girl, stop being so jumpy! It could be anyone calling. A friend of mine. Someone for Ralph—"

Rhoda came back into the room looking at Vonnie. "It's someone asking for you."

Fenella said, "So your friends have caught up with you! Well, that's a good thing!" She got up and stretched her arms in a light, graceful movement. "Uncle Joss, may I take a few of your records upstairs?"

"Of course, you know where they are?"

While their attention was distracted, Vonnie managed to walk towards the door, her legs scarcely seeming to support her. She was vaguely aware of Fenella going out of the far door into the passage that led to the garden room where so recently she herself had played the gramophone.

She felt Rhoda's eyes on her and managed a not very convincing smile.

Out of the sickening, swimming faintness that swirled around her, she heard herself saying, stupidly, unnecessarily, "I'd better go and see who it is—"

She closed the drawing room door carefully behind her, feeling her fingers clammy on the knob. Sunlight flooded through the oriel window over the front door, breaking into green and gold and crimson flame.

A man stood quite still, waiting for her. Vonnie managed to lift her eyes, blinking in the light, and saw Nigel. She opened her lips, but no sound came. She watched his hands move, reaching out to her.

"Vonnie!"

"Don't!" she cried too loudly. "Don't call me by that name! Not here—"

X

Nigel had hold of her hands. Vonnie dragged them away in panic.

"All right," he said quietly. "So we start from scratch! But Vonnie—"

"Not *here*—" her voice was a harsh, desperate whisper. Then, in normal tones, for anyone in the room behind the closed door to hear, she cried, "It's lovely seeing you! We must go somewhere—and talk—" she turned to the drawing room door, opened it and said with exaggerated gaiety, "Uncle Joss, a friend has called unexpectedly. Do you mind if I go out for a while with him?"

"Of course not! Go and enjoy yourself. And if you like, bring him back for a drink later."

She said, "Thank you," closed the door and darted towards the small cloakroom. She dragged her coat from a hanger with hands that shook and ran to the front door and opened it, urging him outside. All these things were done in swift, staccato movements. She could not, unless she had told him outright, have made it more plain that Nigel must not remain in the house a moment longer than necessary!

She ran down the steps, leaving him to close the door.

"And now," Nigel said, walking by her side to the gate, "perhaps I might know what all this mad urgency is about! And why mustn't I call you Vonnie?"

"I'll tell you everything. But first let's get away from the house."

He said, with an attempt at understanding, "Is it that bad, having to live in a place where there's been violent death?"

"It isn't that. I'll explain—"

She was walking quickly, nearly running up the street towards the green vista of trees in Regent's Park. Nigel kept up with her in easy strides.

"I suppose," he said dryly, "there's some sound reason for this panic! But at least tell me—are you glad to see me?"

"Oh, Nigel! I—I am, and—yet I—" She was stammering like a child, emotion again fluttering her. Her hand went out to him and was caught and held.

"Are you staying in the house with Myra?"

"I'm staying with her Uncle Joss Ashlyn," she replied cautiously.

"But when I telephoned a few hours ago and Myra answered she implied that she couldn't put me in touch with you. I gathered you weren't there—in fact that there was some momentous mystery as to where you were! Hey—" he dragged her quickly back. "Don't you know that you cross London roads at special crossings? You'll get killed if you dart across like that!" He kept tight hold of her arm, steered her across the road and into the park.

The evening sun had brushed the grass with golden light; the trees were very still and the lake was like a sheet of gray watered silk. It was quiet at this hour before closing. Most of the children had gone and the people who passed Vonnie, who sat on seats, who walked their dogs, had the unreality of ghosts. Nothing was vital except the realization that life had quite suddenly given her her second chance and whatever happened, she must seize it and hold it because there would never be a third. . . .

There were two chairs set together under a tree.

Vonnie suggested gently, "Let's sit here."

"By all means," Nigel agreed with cool politeness. He took out his cigarette case and offered it to her.

His hand holding the lighter was steady. Hers shook. She didn't look up as she leaned forward a little towards the flame, although she knew his eyes were on her.

"I think," she said and sat back in her chair and gazed ahead of her towards the lake, "you'd better start explanations. You went away, promising to write—"

"I know," he crossed his legs and laid his left hand on his knee.

Vonnie glanced down and saw a scar, livid and red, running the length of the back of his hand.

He nodded, following her gaze.

"It's ugly, isn't it? But they tell me it'll fade in time. It's all part of the reason why I didn't write, Vonnie! Heaven above, don't you think I wanted to? Don't you think it was the most important thing in the world to me?" He turned to her with an almost violent gesture. "Why do you think I was so crazy to find you that I wouldn't accept Myra's dissembling on the telephone? 'Send her a letter care of this address' she told me. 'And I'll see she gets it!' But it was too unsatisfactory—you might not answer that one either! So I fumed for a few hours and at last I couldn't stand it any more. I came around. And there you were and you looked at me as though I were some terrifying ghost and told me not to call you Vonnie. Well—*why?*"

Vonnie watched a gray poodle caper by, heard the heavy-winged flurry of pigeons overhead.

Hold back, her head counseled. *Let him tell his story first!*

She said, as calmly as she could, "Shall we begin *right* at the beginning? Begin with—where you said good-bye and promised to write. Then we'll work up to my explanation."

He hesitated, turning to look at her, his tone suddenly changed and gentle as in their days together in Canada.

"You look just as I've been remembering you! Vonnie, is this the way for us to meet?" His hand touched hers and felt her rejection. "I'm sorry. I suppose after that

125

long silence of mine I can't expect you to fall into my arms! All right!" He had withdrawn his hand, and with a fierce movement he flung his cigarette from him. "It tastes like straw! That's because even a cigarette is poor comfort at a moment like this. Vonnie, was I wrong to try to find you?"

"We must have explanations first," she said with a desperate effort to keep her head. "We can't feel quite the same—until we both know everything—and understand—"

"Until *you* know and understand! There's nothing really on your side for me to know, except of course, why Myra was so mysterious and why you panicked when you saw me. All right, I'll tell you my part of the story."

He paused, leaning forward and clasping his hands between his knees.

Vonnie's glance slid to him; she saw the back of that fair, narrow head, the clear-cut profile with the strong jawline, the broad, well-shaped hands and the livid scar.

"When I left you," Nigel said, staring out at the bright distant lake, "I had to go, as you know, to Yellowknife. I was to drive up there with a man I'd met in a club in Toronto. He was going on business and I partly out of interest and partly because I wanted to be able to tell my firm what was happening up there. We decided we might as well go by road and see a bit of the country. It's pretty wild land up there for the latter part of the way—I guess you don't know it—"

"Only by hearsay."

"Some way out of Yellowknife, the man I was with took a corner too fast. We skidded, hit a fallen tree and somersaulted into scrub. I suppose if a truck hadn't been coming along some ten minutes or so later, we'd both have died from exposure. The van driver went to some mining village nearby and put through a call for help. I don't know how we got to the hospital or quite what happened for some time after that because I'd blacked out. We were both pretty badly smashed up. I had a head injury that blinded me for weeks. In fact, the doctors weren't at all sure they could save my sight. In the end they operated and all was well. I still get bouts of fierce headaches but they'll gradually ease up."

"So that was why I didn't hear!" she cried, turning to him. "But Nigel, I rang up the hotels where you'd been staying in Toronto and Vancouver. They knew nothing!

"No, because my job was finished over here and I went to Yellowknife as a free agent, I no longer had a base in Canada. My London office was cabled and told of the accident and my mother in Deal was also told. Apart from that—well, I was just a stranger in Canada who'd got himself pretty knocked about."

"And you didn't tell the hospital to let me know!" she cried.

"I couldn't, Vonnie. Not till I knew how I was going to react to the operation. If I were going to be blind for the rest of my life, then I'd have to go back to England and start my life all over again, put a steel wall between myself and the past and make a new future."

"And leave me thinking—thinking—"

"That I'd had second thoughts about you? That you were just a very lovely holiday romance? That 'out of sight' was 'out of mind'? Yes, leave you thinking all those things because it would be much easier for you to get over me if you thought I was a pretty poor outsider."

"But you say you wrote to me—"

"So Myra told you that? She told you I'd telephoned today?"

Vonnie let that pass.

"You *did* write?"

"When I was out of danger and knew that my sight was saved, yes, I wrote. But in my half-witted state I put the wrong address on the envelope. My suitcase with my address book in it, everything, was burned in the fire which destroyed the car. As soon as I was able to travel the doctors sent me straight back to Montreal for England. They said seven days' sea voyage would be the best recuperation I could have. I couldn't have come to Vancouver on my own. I was practically carried onto the ship anyway! I told you that in my letter. And while I waited for you to answer, I kept thinking, 'She's on a holiday. The letter will reach her somewhere or other.' I told myself to be patient. Well, I was—too patient! On the very day I left for England, the letter came back to me marked 'Unknown.' When I looked at the envelope I saw the idiotic mistake I'd made. I'd put Vancouver Island on it. You know, I think one of your postal authorities might have used a little gumption and tried Vancouver City. But they didn't—because apparently there is a street of the same name as yours on the Island."

"And you didn't write again?"

"Oh, but I did! The returned letter came when I had only ten minutes to get to the docks. I sent a cable from the ship. I also wrote you two letters—"

"And everything," she said weakly, "is lying in our postbox in the Vancouver apartment!"

"But surely you've got someone out there who'd forward your letters! You don't just shut a place up and disappear."

"I did! I had to. And anyway, I wanted to forget Vancouver and—"

"And me?"

"Since you had gone out of my life, yes." She huddled in her coat. "You're well again, now?"

"More or less. The doctor was right. Those days at sea were the best convalescence I could have had. I told you in my letter that either I must fly out to Vancouver from England a little later to see you and talk about our future, or you must take your courage in both hands and come to London to marry me. And all my fine plans are lying in your postbox in Vancouver!" He reached for her hand.

"You were so wrong not to let me know about the

accident!" she cried shakenly. "It would have saved so much!"

"So much what?"

"Misunderstanding, hurt for me and now explanation—*my* explanation of the rest of the story."

"It isn't easy for a man to know what is the right thing to do," he said. "Don't be too angry! I tried to think of you, Vonnie. But I'd known you only a fortnight. I had no way of being certain whether that was long enough to have your love tested against all odds, even the odds of a man becoming blind! And for God's sake, what a prospect for a girl!"

"If you love someone, you don't look at it that way. If only that letter had reached me!"

"But *I've* reached you now!" he said. "Isn't that even better?"

She dragged her eyes away from his face. Now that it was her turn to explain, she wondered if the fine understanding she had talked about could hold.

"Vonnie, why was Myra so mysterious over the telephone?"

"That wasn't Myra. It was—I—"

"*You?*"

She nodded miserably, without speaking.

"You—on the telephone?" he exploded. She couldn't meet his eyes but she knew that his expression would be as incredulous as his voice. "I don't understand! I ask for you and I'm told—*you* tell me—to write! *You* say you're Myra! What was it? Some game? Or were you so mad at me for that long silence that you were determined not to let me know you were speaking? Was that it, Vonnie?"

She said in a small, taut voice, "Oh no, that wasn't it! I—it was so wonderful hearing your voice. Nigel, it was like heaven opening up."

"I'll say it was! So heavenly, in fact, that you did everything you could to put me off the trail for finding you!"

"If you'd only let me explain!"

"Do, by all means!" he said coldly.

She tried to work out how best to tell him. But in the end the words came unplanned, in swift, jerky phrases, badly strung together. She told him the whole story and she had no way of knowing from his very still, averted head what his reaction was.

"So you see, when you telephoned, I didn't dare to let on who I was! I had to keep up the pretense, though I wanted desperately for you to know I was there. Nigel, you must understand. I'd gone too far in the whole affair to risk discovery at this point. I knew if I told you I was there, speaking to you, you'd come around and demand to see me, call me 'Vonnie.' And then everything would be found out."

"It damned well would!"

The violence of the phrase shook her.

He felt in his pocket and brought out his slim leather cigarette case.

"Perhaps you'd better smoke again."

"No, thank you."

She watched him with a heavy, thudding heart while he snapped open his lighter. The sun was still warm but an inner coldness crept out of her body and made her shiver. She drew her thin coat more closely around her and watched Nigel pocket his lighter.

"Well," he said and breathed out smoke, "you always said you longed to come to England. And you got your way, didn't you?" His voice was hard. "They say if one is determined enough anything is possible. That was quite a scheme you and Myra cooked up, wasn't it?"

The harshness of his comment, his rough choice of words, stunned her. She sat, her face turned towards him, staring into his eyes turned suddenly into a stranger's—cold and remote as ice.

"I wanted to come to England, yes," she began waveringly, "but—"

"And so you seized your opportunity," he cut in, his voice holding a cold hard mockery. "Clever girl!"

"I've told you the truth," she said simply. "I've even tried to explain exactly how I argued it all out to myself. *Why* I came. You must see it wasn't just that I seized an opportunity I couldn't otherwise have afforded, to come to England."

"Whether I see it or not appears to be immaterial. You came—and it's landed you slap into a nice mess, hasn't it?"

"Yes, it has," she retorted, whipping herself to defiance to meet his unexpected anger—"and I didn't expect you to understand! Nor did I expect you to behave like my accuser! I haven't harmed *you*."

"So it's not my affair, and I should shake my head at you and smile indulgently and say, 'Naughty girl!' But what does it matter to me how you lie and cheat so long as you're having fun!"

"Fun! In a house where someone has died violently!"

A shadow of something like contrition swept his face. "I'm sorry. I shouldn't have said that. It was in pretty bad taste."

"You shouldn't have said any of the things you have!" she retorted, anger warring with cold, sick fear inside herself. "I've told you that what I did was mostly for Joss Ashlyn's and Myra's sake. Whether you believe me or not, that's the truth! And if you *don't* believe me, then there's nothing more to be said between us!"

She waited. Nigel drew on his cigarette, blew a coil of smoke out into the soft evening air, and remained silent. Vonnie clenched her hands, hurting her palms with her nails. She could have struck at him in an impotent urge for him to speak.

"You've taken all this trouble to track me down," she cried at last unable to bear the silence. "And now that I've told you everything you won't even try to understand!"

"I understand!" he cried in a low, furious tone. "Like

131

blazes I do! You and your friend Myra are making a fool of an old man!"

"We're not!" She leaned back in her chair, forcing herself to steadiness, to remember that this was a man she loved . . . and who loved her. Determined to find her, he had heard her story, and having done so could give only blame and criticism. *This is my fine dream of a love that has trust and faith in it!*

The low, brilliant sun had moved clear of the tree and dazzled her eyes; people passed, but she was unaware of them save as shadows. *This* was her private world—this one in the demon's circle of two chairs and a plane tree. This, with Nigel so near her—and yet in understanding as far from her as if they were strangers wearing masks. . . .

She realized, with a sick jolt, that Nigel was saying something to her, his voice low and without emphasis.

"When I spoke to you on the telephone, you kept up the pretense—"

"I've tried to explain. I *had* to! There were people around!"

"—to *me!*" he continued as though she hadn't spoken. "You talked as Myra."

"I talked as no one in particular! Have you never been so shocked that your brain didn't act? Have you never done or said something wild or foolish just because you are so shaken you can't think straight? So you say the wrong thing, act idiotically and against your own impulses because shock has made you numb and stupid and unable to think quickly enough?"

There was no answer.

"Oh, no," she studied the hard, remote profile by her side. "You wouldn't do that, would you? *You'd never* lose your head! But *I* did! Hearing your voice made my mind somersault. It was the most wonderful thing—and yet I was trapped. I couldn't think quickly enough what to say to you to make you realize that I was Vonnie and at the same time guard what I said from the people who might be listening."

He was watching some ducks drifting over the rippled lake, their feathers opalescent in the sunshine.

"So you denied me. Oh yes," as she started to protest, "that's what it amounted to. You hadn't the slightest intention of letting me know you were here in London! 'Write,' you said. 'Write and I'll see she gets the letter!' 'Send in your application for her love, Mr. Foster, and the matter will be dealt with!' " His voice taunted her.

Vonnie said, in a whisper, "Please may I have a cigarette?"

He gave her one and lit it without raising his eyes to her face. She leaned back, drawing in smoke, trying to steady herself. Behind his anger, she guessed, was hurt. He had dialed the number of the St. John's Wood house with such wild hope, such joy that at last he could find her again. And she, at the other end, with her world suddenly topsy-turvy, had denied him. She tried to put herself into his place, to see the whole affair as he would. *But I'd understand!* And if I didn't, at least I'd hold back my condemnation. I'd try, I'd try so hard to understand because I loved and loving is trust!

Nigel was looking away so that all she saw was the back of the fair head. The *proud,* fair head! That was what separated them, pride and hurt. Nigel's, not hers. But then she was not a man; she could not argue from a masculine outlook. That was the tragedy, she thought, between people who loved—the utter inability of the sexes to see things from the same angle.

She spoke gently. "If I hurt you, Nigel, I'm sorry. But believe me, it was the most wonderful thing in the world to hear your voice."

"But not wonderful enough, was it? Much, very much stronger than that emotion was the realization that here I was, someone out of your past, all blindly and in utter innocence raring to spoil your beautiful plan! And then, I plunge a dagger even more dangerously into your lovely masquerade because I came around myself to see what had happened to the girl I was looking for. I dared to use her name!"

"Have you ever flown thousands of miles, only to walk into a strange house and find—a murder?" she demanded.

"I've said that part was very dreadful for you! But it's divorced from your actions. You didn't know when you made your plans what you were walking into. Your deception and the Ashlyn murder are entirely separate." He turned his head and looked directly into her eyes, his own intense, sun-flecked. "For God's sake, *I'm Nigel!* We said we loved one another out in Vancouver!"

"And you went away. Oh, I know what happened. But I didn't at the time. All these weeks I thought—well, you know perfectly well what I thought! I tried to put you out of my mind—I hoped I'd end by forgetting or, at least, by being able to think of you without being hurt. That's all a woman can do when a man says he loves her and then vanishes from her life."

"So, Vonnie?"

"So," she cried with spirit, "you did a foolish thing in not letting me know you were injured, in not believing in my love enough to know that whatever happened, I loved you. Well, *I* did a foolish thing on the telephone— for a different reason. Because I couldn't make the right split-second decision as to what to say to you. We both did something foolish, Nigel—you as well as I—"

"But *I* didn't deceive! I wonder," he added, "if I ever really knew you during those two weeks in Vancouver? Or whether all that was playacting, too?"

"You won't believe, will you, that someone can do a wrong thing from a right motive?" she protested wearily.

"Believe? I don't know what to believe about you!"

It was hopeless for her to find some common ground. Frustration beat about her so that she felt her temples throb, her face burn with the futile frantic effort not to cry with rage.

"All right," her voice shuddered in the quiet green and

gold of the emptying park. "You can't understand and you prefer not to give me the benefit of the doubt! I'm a cheat and a liar according to you! Well, then, there's nothing more to say, is there?" Somewhere above them, birds twittered and protested sleepily from a nest. Vonnie's coat had dropped open and the pleats of her blue dress splayed out like a fan of silk.

They had reached an *impasse* and there seemed nothing more to say. She dropped the half smoked cigarette she had taken and let him light, scarcely realizing that she had done so, reached out her foot and stamped violently on it, and kicked the stub into the grass with the toe of her shoe.

Nothing more to say? But there *was*.

"Perhaps," she said in a hoarse, choked voice, "you'd like to go to Myra's uncle and tell him what I've told you. Perhaps rigid truth is more important to you than compassion?"

"Whatever I feel, don't worry! You're safe. I won't betray you."

"But you can't understand—or forgive?"

"It's so outrageous," he said violently, "that it sickens me!"

"How righteous you are!" she mocked, wanting to hurt. "How wonderful it must be to have such rigid principles that you can play God!" She gathered her thin coat around her and rose.

Immediately Nigel was standing in front of her. His fingers gripped her arms.

"How long did you say you were going to keep up this—masquerade?"

"For a month. Just one month out of a lifetime! Then I shall go back to Canada and Joss Ashlyn will be happy and Myra, I hope, will have become engaged to Brad. She loves him. And everyone will be happy. Even *I*—" she said defiantly, "will be glad I did what I did!"

"You little fool!" he shook her.

She dragged herself away.

"Everything that happens is a matter of personal opinion. Even a thing like this. I'm not being foolish or evil —not in my own mind. And, whatever anyone thinks, that's what really matters—one's own conscience!"

"Hasn't it occurred to you that long before the month is out someone's going to find out?" he almost shouted at her. "Something will happen—you'll make a false move, or some twist of circumstance will reveal the truth. Then where do you stand? Where will this Joss Ashlyn's and Myra's happiness be then?"

"Nothing will happen to spoil it, I shall be careful."

"I'm damn sure you will!" he said roughly. "But not careful enough! Your forget that you've become indirectly involved with the police over a murder. You've no idea the trouble they go to to smoke out lies!"

Suddenly Vonnie knew that if she stayed she would break down. Then Nigel would think, "Tears, the last resource of a woman!" And that wouldn't help her, either! Without understanding, love was a mockery. That was the fundamental truth.

She turned with a sudden instinct for escape and began to run.

She had no idea whether Nigel was watching her or not as she went blindly down the path.

Reaching the street she managed somehow to cross the road safely. Then she tore down the avenue and through the gate of Joss Ashlyn's house. She stumbled up the steps, ringing the bell with a shaking finger.

Fenella opened the door almost immediately.

She said, with raised eyebrows, "I saw you from the dining room, racing down the road. Don't tell me you were running from reporters or news photographers!"

Vonnie leaned against the closed door and shook her head.

"Then what's happened?"

Fenella watched her, still breathing hard, hang up her coat in the little cloakroom off the hall.

"You know, you'd better come in and sit down. You're

shaking like a leaf! Myra, what's scared you? Did you meet some thugs in the park?"

Vonnie took a chance on the truth. She said, still panting, "Someone I knew in Canada called. We went for a walk—and—we quarreled. That's all."

" 'All'!" Fenella demanded shrewdly. "It looks as though it were everything!"

"I suppose I took it hard, coming on top of everything else."

"You're a fiend for welcoming difficulties, aren't you?" Fenella said. "Here you have Uncle Joss's own suggestion that you should stay in a hotel, away from this horrible murder house, and you choose to stay. Then you meet up with some boyfriend over here and straight away quarrel. Oh well, come on out into the garden. We're all there. Ralph too." Fenella put up a hand and lifted a dark wing of hair from her forehead as though she were hot. "Men can be the devil, but there you are! We'd be bored without them!"

Vonnie said vaguely, "I'll join you presently. But I'm hot. I'll go up and wash my face. I'll feel better then," and turned and escaped.

In her room, she ran water in the washbasin and plunged her face in it. The shock of the cold water revived her a little and drying herself, she wandered to the window. She could see them all in the garden, sitting just below the terrace. Rhoda was there with them, Fenella came down the steps and Ralph rose. She saw their hands touch for a moment and their gaze hold. Joss was fanning flies away with a rolled-up newspaper. Rhoda watched Fenella. Seen from a distance—too far away to read expressions in eyes, to note suspicions chase like shadows across faces—the scene was so calm. It was like a summer idyll with the moths already fluttering under the trees and the flowers dry and hot and brilliant.

Vonnie turned away and her gaze caught the picture on the wall. She crossed the room, lifted shaking hands and took it down. She opened the built-in wardrobe and dragging up a chair, laid the picture on the top shelf. Old Joss would probably never come into the room, and if Rhoda noticed, Vonnie would say quite honestly that it reminded her too vividly of an unhappy love affair in her life.

XI

FOR THE WHOLE of the following day, which was Monday, thunder threatened.

Vonnie moved through the heavy atmosphere of that morning slowly, listlessly, as though age had settled on her mind and body. She had had her second chance to make everything right between herself and Nigel and had failed. Useless to tell herself that she had really tried and could have done no better. The fact remained that her futile efforts had proved the bitter, inescapable fact that their love had no depth. It was over because it had never been real. The explanations that should have drawn them closer had been like some great cleft which nothing could bridge.

After dinner, Joss Ashlyn switched on the television, pulled the settee around to an angle of his liking and sprawled, legs straight before him, to look in on a political discussion.

Vonnie couldn't rest. English politics was like a foreign language she had no desire to learn. She wandered up to her room to get a book and heard symphony music coming from Rhoda's room. Ralph had not returned home yet and Fenella was not expected this evening. Vonnie went down into the garden room, curled up on the wide cushioned window seat and tried to read. But the words seemed to run into one another with her inability to concentrate and presently she gave up, closing the book and leaving it there on the table.

She wandered out into the garden. The thundery airlessness pressed down on her and the dun clouds were almost stationary; in the distance thunder growled. The flowers had a wilting brilliance and the thick creamy magnolia petals were as luminous as moonlight in the livid glow from the sky.

Sitting down on the grass she hugged her knees. Around her were the flat gray backs of the other houses, their façades broken up by the foreground of the heavy, leafy fan shapes of the trees. But again, as she sat there, she had a sensation of eyes watching her from those distant windows, wondering about her . . . recalling her name in the newspapers they had read that Sunday. Myra Ashlyn, the girl from Canada who has walked in upon a murder. . . .

She laid her face on her knees and looked down into the short dry grass. Tiny insects stirred the blades, scuttling light as feathers, in search of food.

A sound from somewhere above her caused her to look up. Ralph was closing the top window—the attic window from which she had seen the light flash on and off on that fatal evening. Had it been Ralph there on the night Felix Ashlyn died? Had he heard the fall of a heavy man and the crashing of glass? Had they been his footsteps she had heard coming down the front steps? Ralph walking calmly out of that house, knowing perfectly well that something had happened that should be investigated? But, out of disinterest or cowardice or guilt —escaping?

He saw Vonnie and waved. She made no acknowledgement and turned her head away, staring at the livid sky.

Where was Nigel at this moment? She felt her senses melt and swim at the thought of him and pulled herself together. Forget Nigel! He's in the past and no good was ever done to anyone by remembering unhappy things. A page was turned and only fools looked back. . . .

"Hello! You can't stargaze yet, the sky's too light!"

Vonnie looked around, startled. Ralph crossed the lawn

140

and flung himself down by her side. He leaned on one elbow smiling at her.

"I'm not trespassing," he assured her. "Your uncle has given me permission to use the garden. It's charming, isn't it?" he glanced about him. "That magnolia tree is lovely."

"It is," she agreed.

"Odd," he turned and looked at her speculatively. "How people change. You have! Your hair used to be dark red, Titian colored."

A thread of alarm rippled through her.

"How do you know that?"

"I've seen the portrait your uncle did of you when you were a little girl of four or five. You were standing in front of the magnolia and you're wearing a white dress with ruffles around the neck. Do you remember being painted?"

She said honestly, "No."

"Would you like to see it?" He sat forward, one hand braced on the lawn, ready to jump up.

"No," Vonnie said again, sharply this time.

"Why not? I thought you'd find it fun to see yourself as a very little girl. It's an enchanting painting."

She said firmly, "I don't think Uncle would like us to go wandering in his studio. He has already said he doesn't have visitors in there."

"But we're different. He wouldn't mind a bit. In fact, I'll ask him first."

"Thank you, but I don't want to go into that room."

He said kindly, "I understand. Then, if you like, I'll bring the portrait out here—asking your uncle first, of course. You really *should* see it."

"Some other time!" she looked up at the sky. "There's going to be a storm, anyway."

"We can stay here till it rains. It's cooler than in the house. You know, Myra, some time or other I'd like to talk to you about Canada."

"Of course. I'll tell you anything you want to know." She was thankful for the change of conversation.

"I've often thought of emigrating. Canada sounds, from everything I've ever read, to be my sort of country. Fine cities; beautiful, unspoiled country. I'd love to ski and skate in the winter and swim in the summer —the summers here aren't nearly hot enough for me."

"Well, if you went east, say to Montreal or Toronto you'd know what hot summers really were," she laughed. "But there everyone has a weekend cottage by the lakes or up in the Laurentians if they live in Montreal, so the heat doesn't worry them so much."

"It would be a matter of whether I'd find a job out there. Advertising's a cutthroat game."

"Funny," Vonnie said dreamily, staring into the distance, "how people always think somewhere else is better than where they are! *I'd* love to live in London forever. I wouldn't mind the climate. There's something exciting about it—and it's a different excitement from New York where the air is stimulating. It's the excitement of tradition and the famous people who always seem to find their way here at some time or other, and the nearness to Europe." She paused and then said doubtfully, "I wonder how Fenella would like Canada?"

"Fenella?" he echoed is surprise.

"Well, you and she—" Vonnie began. Then she stopped and felt herself color with embarrassment. "I'm sorry, I shouldn't have said that. But I thought—"

"If I go to Canada, I go alone."

"But I thought—I mean—" She stopped aghast at her further tactlessness. "I seem to have spoken out of turn. I really *am* sorry!"

"It's all right," he said quietly, "but I think I'd better give you a little explanation. After all, you're living here. If you don't know how things stand, then you may drop quite a number of bricks—"

"You're right!" she said ruefully. "I'd forgotten the basic social teaching. 'When in doubt, say nothing'!"

"Fenella and I have known each other for about two years. We're friends, that's all. There's not the slightest hint of anything more between us." His eyes met Vonnie's, smiled for a moment and then faltered.

Vonnie picked up a blade of grass and ran it through her fingers. There was nothing to add. What Ralph had said had been firm and final—and a lie. . . . Of that she was certain. At some time or other during the two years they had known one another, there had most certainly been more than friendship between them. In fact, remembering their long, significant glances at moments in conversation, Vonnie was quite certain that the change in their relationship, if change there was, was recent—too recent in fact to be entirely accepted by either.

Why had Ralph lied to her? Was he afraid that if Fenella really wanted him, she would not let him go? Was that why he had been asking about Canada? Ralph was weaker than Fenella, and he knew that the only way he could escape her was to leave the country. Fenella might follow him, if she so chose, to Paris or Rome. She was intelligent but not knowledgeable. To her Canada was still the "back of beyond" and not the place for her. If Ralph wanted to free himself from her, it was his best possible way of escape.

But was it Fenella he needed to escape from or something else? Something that haunted him? A murder. . . .

"You know," Ralph said leaning forward and peering at her, "it was Fenella who found your portrait tucked away among a heap at the back of the studio. I remember she said you were much prettier than she was when you were a child and that that was one of the things she hated you for. She said she'd almost forgotten what you looked like and as we looked at the portrait together she said what curious smoky-violet eyes you had. But they aren't. They're golden brown!"

Vonnie let the blade of grass flutter onto the lawn and laid her hands in her lap.

"Uncle Joss probably thought smoky-violet, as you call

them, more glamorous to paint than brown." She passed off the explanation with simulated ease, not daring to meet Ralph's candid, questioning eyes, "I expect he just made me prettier than I really was!"

"He tells me that he always made a point in his portraits of keeping as faithfully as he could to a likeness. It's old-fashioned, these days, he says. But that was *his* way in his time—and a lot of success it brought him!"

Thunder rolled, a little nearer this time. Vonnie glanced apprehensively at the sky.

Ralph said, "You know, you must let me take you around a little. You've seen nothing of London yet but Regent's Park!"

Vonnie said, cautiously, "Thank you. Perhaps sometime—" and then, quite deliberately, "Where's Fenella?"

"Oh, she's gone to some girl's supper party to talk over clothes for a wedding. She's to be a bridesmaid."

Someone was at the upstairs landing window. Vonnie recognized the neat head and the dark dress and wondered how long Rhoda had been watching them.

She thought: Everyone here is watching everyone else . . . as though no one is quite trusted! Perhaps that was the inevitable way in a house of mystery and violence. Perhaps you began to ask yourself if the most trustworthy, the one with the most candid eyes, had fooled you all the time!

She stirred and looked up at the sky again.

"I think I feel rain."

"It won't be here for some time yet. Thunder clouds move as slowly as elephants! Don't worry. And, Myra, I like talking to you."

Vonnie did not take her eyes from the great bank of cloud that rose like a backcloth for the immobile trees.

"Ralph!"

"Yes?"

"What do you think about Uncle Felix's murder?"

She sensed his dislike of her question. But after a pause, he answered quietly enough, "I think, as the police do—and Fenella does not—that the brandy was meant for your Uncle Joss."

"And that someone outside the house was responsible?"

"Of course."

She turned, protesting with sudden intensity.

"But no one who is really near him could have done that awful thing! Everyone here is dreadfully upset about it. He—inspires a sort of reluctant love, so—"

"Never go by appearances, Myra; if you do you are in for shocks. People aren't in the least what they seem."

For a stark moment she stared at him with a terrified suspicion that somehow or other he knew about her. Then as she saw him smile she relaxed, saying in a perfectly normal voice, "I won't believe Uncle Joss has an enemy in this house!"

Ralph did not answer. Vonnie saw a shadow cross his face, at once secretive and fearful. Some inner urge forced her to insist where she knew insistence was unwelcome.

"Do *you* think the—the murderer is here?"

He avoided her eyes.

"Leave it, Myra? Leave conjecture. You're a stranger here. Be glad it's that way and you're not concerned. There are things here—undercurrents, best not explored."

"If you feel them, why do you stay?"

He shrugged his shoulders.

"You don't know what it's like trying to get a flat in London these days. Besides—"

"Besides what?"

"You're nice and honest and uncomplicated," he flashed his smile at her. "Stay that way. And don't probe too much because that way lies danger."

You're honest and uncomplicated! But I'm not! I'm acting a lie and *there* lies the danger! I'm the least honest person here in this house! Or am I? Isn't there perhaps one even less honest than I? The murderer. . . .

If Ralph knew there was danger, did that mean he

guessed who killed Felix Ashlyn? Why did he not go to the police with his suspicions?

In the pause in their conversation, another thought struck her with a sick thrust at her heart. Suppose Ralph were in some oblique way warning her against himself! Suppose he were the killer and, liking her, did not want her to place herself in a position where she might be in danger from him?

But he could not have killed Felix Ashlyn or intended to kill old Joss. Why should he? What reason in the world would this young man, a stranger to the family until two years ago, have to kill a man who was nothing to him?

She brushed her dress down and jumped to her feet.

Ralph, too, leaped up with a graceful, almost a dancer's movement.

He said, looking at her and smiling, "Haven't you any friends in London to take you out of all this? Visitors from the Commonwealth always seem to have connections here, particularly someone like you, British by birth."

"I suppose I could look up a few—" she said reluctantly.

"I'd ferret them out if I were you, Myra," he urged her. "This is no house for a visitor to stay cooped up in!"

(A visitor who asks too many questions?)

She said, lightly chiding, "I've only just come! Give me time to get my breath and sort myself out!"

"You did have one friend look you up yesterday, didn't you?"

"Yes." She began to walk towards the steps to the house.

"I was coming downstairs when you were in the hall. You know, Myra," he fell into step by her side. "Funny thing, I could have sworn he called you 'Vonnie.' But that's the name of the girl you share a flat with, isn't it?"

She paused, apparently to look at the magnolia flowers, and put out her hand to touch one pale petal.

"I suppose he thought you were both over here," Ralph

continued. "He must have been expecting to see Vonnie and had quite a shock when you walked into the hall."

That was a let-out! she thought, and with relief, managed a laugh.

"Yes, that's what happened."

"Well, at least, if he's here in England, I hope he'll take you around. Or would your friend Vonnie be jealous?"

She said in a small frozen voice, "I don't suppose I'll ever see him again," and walked up the steps into the garden room.

At the door she paused, the matter of the light in the attic still nagging at her.

"I wonder if it's true that no one was here when Uncle Felix died?"

The words seemed to echo in the sparsely furnished room.

Ralph stopped walking and stood still. As she turned, looking at him half over her shoulder, he said, "If there had been, then maybe his life could have been saved."

"But suppose someone *was* here and heard the fall and—didn't go down to see—"

Did she imagine the swift, small gleam in his eyes, like an alert?

"Why shouldn't they, Myra? Unless they had something to hide—some knowledge—"

"That's what I mean."

"You mean Rhoda might have come back, don't you?"

"Or someone—"

"Rhoda is the only possibility. Your uncle was out and so was I."

"I suppose," she said, "the police wanted your alibis."

"Why, Myra!" he flashed. And then he managed a thin laugh. "You've been reading too many American thrillers where some clever amateur solves a murder mystery! But this is reality. Leave it to the police, my dear!"

"I'm—interested," she said unabashed. "After all, as I

didn't know Uncle Felix I can't be expected to be heart-broken and so, as I'm plunged into a sort of—orbit of murder, naturally I want to talk about it."

"Anything we can say has been said. The rest is conjecture. It's better to let it be."

"But *did* the police want alibis?"

He leaned against the iron railing of the small terrace and surveyed her.

"You really do flog a subject, don't you? Yes, we gave alibis, but in this case they mean nothing. The drug was in the bottle; the murderer could be miles away when the fatal dose was drunk. This is a case where it might be more convincing *not* to have an alibi!"

"Then I don't see how they'll ever find out anything—"

"Except the chance that whoever was seen in the garden that night might have been watching the house, hanging around waiting for Felix to—well, to put it bluntly—drop dead!"

She shivered.

"But it was dark, and the maid next door and the woman in the house across the garden couldn't possibly see whoever was there clearly enough to describe her."

"You've no idea how clever the police are in building up the truth on the slenderest clues!"

"But they can't make an arrest on a vague description. It's just not possible!" She was protesting too much! She forced herself to add, lightly, "They're not magicians!"

"Don't you be too certain! Police methods, plodding, sifting and clever psychology can produce even magic results. I wouldn't be surprised if they didn't question *you* again! Ask to see your passport, get proof of your time of arrival in this country."

She caught her breath in a sharp involuntary gasp.

"But there'd be no reason! I didn't know Uncle Felix."

"Of course you didn't! I'm only just showing you how thorough they are in their investigations. Outrageous ideas are followed, not because in themselves they'd lead anywhere, but because maybe, through them, another little piece could be fitted into the jigsaw. Hey!" He put out a hand and touched hers. His fingers closed tentatively over hers. "Don't look like that! You're innocent, so they can't hurt you. The very worst would be that you'd have to give proof of your arrival on Saturday, and offer up your passport."

"I wish I had never come!" The words were torn raggedly from her.

"I know! It's wretched for you. But Myra, you're the one person in this house who doesn't have to be afraid of suspicion. The rest of us—"

"But you scarcely knew Uncle Felix, either, did you?"

"I live in this house; I'm a friend of the family. And remember, the police believe he died by mistake. They are quite certain the drug was meant for your Uncle Joss."

"Even so—" He had opened up the way. Now it was for her to lead him on, to watch and listen hard and try to find the slightest giveaway that would prove he had been in the house when Felix Ashlyn died.

"Even so, my dear," he said softly, "the police won't think I'm entirely without motive." He paused. She had decided that he could only be in his early thirties, but suddenly he aged. There were strained, taut lines about his mouth; his eyes lost their amused brightness and became clouded and tired. He lifted a hand and ran it over his smooth hair. "You may as well hear it from me as from anyone."

"Hear—what?"

"The truth! About Fenella and me. What I told you before was a bit of a lie. There was a time when we thought we could make a go of things. But it didn't work out."

"Marry, you mean?"

"Yes."

She waited. The house and the garden were very quiet; somewhere very far away there was music.

"If the police think that there is still something between Fenella and me," Ralph said, "then I have a motive, haven't I? You'd better face it, Myra! If Mr. Ashlyn was to be an uncle by marriage—a rich uncle at that —I wouldn't be entirely lacking in personal interest, would I?"

Of course not, she thought. A rich old man—a sick man—and a will that perhaps left the major part of his money to Fenella. Fenella and Ralph. Oh, she saw!

"But, you inferred that it's all over between you."

"All over and yet not all over!" his voice held bitterness. "The rest of the story is Fenella's. Don't ask me any more." He turned and walked away from her, back down the steps, disappearing around the side of the house while she stood there, consumed with curiosity, and uncertain in her suspicion of him.

All over—and yet not all over? She leaned against the sun-warmed wall and worked it out. One of them had cooled off. But which one? Fenella? If so, then there was no question of suspicion for murder against Ralph. He would have no reason for wishing either of the elderly Ashlyn men dead because he would have nothing to gain. Then had Ralph himself called their affair off? Ralph breaking with Fenella while she still loved him?

It still made nonsense of his involvement. . . .

There was some other explanation then, and one that eluded her.

"Let it be!" Ralph had said, "because this way lies danger."

But she couldn't let it be. Curiosity was the oldest stimulus in the world. Pandora had opened the sealed box and evil had escaped. . . .

XII

THE INQUEST was over. To her relief, Vonnie was told that it was not necessary for her to appear. But when they returned, she sat listening to the discussion of the ordeal in the courtroom and realized that the relentless search for a killer would still go on. The inquest merely set the seal on the hunt.

Each time Vonnie passed the studio on the way to the garden, the door had been closed. Then, on the morning after the inquest, just before going out to spend the day in the West End of London, she went downstairs to test the weather.

She was wearing the blue suit Myra had given her, but it was silk and might possibly be too thin for this cloudy day.

Passing the studio, and finding the door open for the first time, she paused and looked in. Then curiosity overcame her and she entered the great room.

The north light rendered the studio almost shadowless. Paintings were stacked against the walls, and on the dais stood an antique gilded chair with lions' claw arms.

She stood and looked about her.

Great panes of stained glass, some of them an inch thick and most of them looking very dusty, were piled on the floor—their colors rich crimson and dark gold, emerald and royal purple. A trestle table was covered with pieces cut into irregular facets. One or two finished panels stood around, their brilliant designs, some abstract, some of saints, embedded not in lead, but in the

151

more modern medium of cement. A table was set with the instruments of the stained glass worker. The studio where a great artist had painted the portraits of the rich and famous was now a workshop for an old man with an absorbing and beautiful hobby.

Vonnie wandered around and for a moment forgot that this was a room where a man had died. Death did not seem part of this lofty room with its wall and half roof of glass.

"Are you looking for something, Myra?"

The voice came so sharply in the intense quiet that Vonnie jumped.

Rhoda came through the door.

"I'm sorry," Vonnie said quickly. "Am I trespassing?"

"No—not exactly.

"I found the door open and I couldn't resist looking in. It wasn't morbid curiosity about a death here—I just wanted to see the room in which Uncle Joss has worked all these years. And all this stained glass—it's—lovely, isn't it?" She began to feel embarrassment at Rhoda's cool gaze flicking over her, assessing, it seemed, her hair, her face, her clothes.

She said, lightly, "I actually came down to see what the weather was like outside. If it was cold or not. I thought I'd have a day in town and then lunch out somewhere and perhaps go to the Tate Gallery this afternoon."

"It's a good idea. Where will you lunch?"

"I don't know. I was going to ask you if you could tell me of a place that is nice but not too expensive."

Rhoda named a few places—a hotel, a restaurant, a store.

"Take your pick," she said in a voice that did not seem to be quite concerned with what she was saying. "Oh, and—just a moment, I'll fetch a small map I have; it'll go nicely in your handbag and wherever you are you'll be able to get your bearings from it."

She was gone only a minute. When she returned she

gave Vonnie the map. There was something else in her hand. She glanced at Vonnie's suit.

"I don't think you are warmly enough dressed. There's a cool wind," she paused and added conversationally, "That's a very beautiful suit. I haven't seen it before. You didn't by any chance buy it over here?"

"It was bought in a store in Canada."

Rhoda's eyes were focused fascinatedly on the coat.

"How strange!"

"What is?"

"Well, the buttons are so unusual," she came a little nearer, studying them. "Raised glass with those tiny birds painted in the center. They must be handmade."

"The suit wasn't cheap." Vonnie laughed remembering what Myra had paid for it, "so the buttons may be unique. I wouldn't know."

Rhoda held out her left hand, opened her palm and said, "And this one is identical!"

It was a small rounded glass button with, in the center, a tiny brightly-painted chaffinch.

Rhoda's gaze moved to Vonnie.

"Each bird on the buttons of your coat is different, isn't it? A robin, a blackbird, a budgerigar and dove. You haven't got one like this—"

"I suppose whoever painted them had an order for dozens and I just didn't get the chaffinch," she said cheerfully.

"It *is* strange—" Rhoda's light eyes regarded her speculatively. "You see, I found this."

"Did you?" Vonnie asked. "Then someone will be mad about that because he probably can't match them!"

"I found it," Rhoda continued as though Vonnie hadn't spoken, "outside by the rhododendron bushes at the side of the house."

Nothing could have stopped Vonnie's sudden involuntary gesture with her hand. It darted to her pocket and withdrew again.

153

She tried to keep her voice even, tried to hold on to the polite, barely interested expression on her face.

"So, they're not as uncommon as I thought!"

"They can't be, can they, Myra?"

Rhoda was watching her with the bland, incomprehensible stare of a cat.

Hands tightly at her side, Vonnie said, "I suppose things get carried accidentally from one garden to another. Dustmen, for instance, or—even birds. Do you have jackdaws in England? I believe they're terrible thieves."

"It's heavy," Rhoda said briefly, "and shiny and would be difficult for a bird to carry. No, there must be some other explanation as to why it was there. That unknown woman the maid next door saw in the garden, for instance."

"Of course." Too eagerly Vonnie agreed.

"Oh, well, perhaps I'd better keep it. Someone may come asking for it." The hand closed over the bright, pretty thing. Rhoda's arm dropped to her side. "I should take an umbrella with you, if I were you. And I must get on with my chores," she said, in a changed voice, turning to the door. "Take care those buttons of yours are secure. You see how easily one can lose them!" It was her smiling, parting shot.

Vonnie stood where she was, sick with the sudden fear that had crept too near her. For she knew without a doubt that the button was hers. She remembered how, when Myra had given her this suit, there had been an extra button sewn to a piece of cloth. But the stitching had become undone and Vonnie had slipped the extra button unthinkingly into the pocket of the short coat, meaning to put it away somewhere safely, and forgetting.

She had worn the suit when she had come to look at the house on the night she arrived. She had chosen it because it was dark in color and would help her to be inconspicuous. She recalled how, hiding in the bushes, she had suddenly realized how white her hands might show against the light that had flashed on suddenly in an upstairs window and how she had thrust her hands in her pockets. She had taken them out again to shoo away the black cat which was showing her too much attention. That was when she must have been too absorbed in keeping herself invisible to notice that she had dragged the button out of her pocket and dropped it.

And now the little ornamental thing with the chaffinch painted on it could easily destroy all her careful plans. A button could involve her in a murder, prove her an impostor, bring disgrace on Myra and hurt Uncle Joss....

Rhoda could not possibly guess that she had arrived in England earlier than expected and that it had been she in the garden. The fact remained, however, that she knew perfectly well that such buttons were unique; she knew too that Vonnie had not worn that suit since she had been here.

Suppose, she thought, I admitted that I find I have lost my spare button? Suppose I say that I had it in my handbag and must have dropped it sometime going along that path? That was the sort of reply she should have thought of at the time. Now it was too late. Better to pretend to forget all about it and show only a casual interest. Yet, remembering Rhoda's curious cat-like gaze, she had a shaken suspicion that this was not the end of the affair.

Rhoda would hand it to the police.

And Inspector Vachell would come and ask to see the women's clothes, would compare the button with the ones on Vonnie's suit. And then?

Well, what? Ralph had said that the police were like magicians, they placed a lot of most insignificant facts in a hat—and pulled out the complete story of a crime.

Perhaps Rhoda would keep quiet.

Every instinct mocked at that! Rhoda was an enigma, she might want someone suspected—and convicted. *Want it for her own sake* because she was as suspect as everyone else in the house? But why should Rhoda want to kill old Joss Ashlyn? For the same reason as anyone else in the house! *Because someone here knew the terms of his will....* Just one? Or all of them?

XIII

IT WAS ONE thing to make up your mind to put someone out of your life, but quite another to carry it out. Strength of will was puny when measured against regrets and longings and love! The conversation in the park with Nigel had become a kind of haunting background to whatever Vonnie did, and wherever she was.

In moments when she succeeded in forgetting, such little things brought the whole disastrous memory back. Flowers in a shop window. (When he found that she loved yellow roses, Nigel had searched Vancouver for them.) . . . Books displayed in a shop window. (They had both declared their preference for travel books. "If I can't visit a place, then at least I can wallow in someone else's description!" "I want to go to Tehran and Istanbul and Damascus," she had said.) . . . A cinema showing a film she had seen with Nigel in Vancouver. ("Danny Kaye 'magics' me!" she had declared laughing.)

Vonnie took the days in both hands, determined to squeeze them dry of activity, to wrench memory out once and for all. She was free to come and go. Each day she chose to stay out to lunch, old Joss encouraging her and Rhoda suggesting a place for her to eat.

On Thursday Vonnie would be near Soho and Rhoda told her of a little Italian restaurant in Charlotte Street where she would not feel too awkward eating alone.

"It's not cheap but the food is lovely. The place gets booked up, so you'd better book a table. I'll ring for you, if you like."

"Thank you."

At one o'clock Vonnie walked up Charlotte Street looking for Au Petit Bretagne.

She found it, seemingly small and insignificant with a narrow doorway and a swinging sign outside. The thick green leaves and tall stems of potted plants spiraled up the window as though advertising a heated jungle. But when Vonnie went through the revolving door, she found it cool inside. A waiter took her along the aisle of little tables, packed closely together, to one at the far end.

But there was no empty table there. "I suppose I shall share," she thought and then the eyes of a man at one of the tables lifted and met hers and everything went wild and spinning around her.

The waiter paused. The man rose as though he had been expecting her.

She said, faintly, "Nigel!" and sat down weakly in the chair the head waiter held out.

"I'm sorry to spring myself on you like this. But I had to see you," he broke off and looked up at the waiter. "Drink? Oh yes, yes please. What'll you have, Vonnie?"

She chose a martini and only later realized that she didn't like them much. Her brain was somersaulting, at one minute on the peak of hope that this was capitulation, because Nigel had said "I had to see you!" Then, plunging down because it wasn't love she saw in his eyes, but a kind of flashing urgency.

"Cigarette?"

"Thank you."

She took one and over the strike and flare of the match, she was silently posing questions. But she couldn't ask them. She waited for moments that seemed eternal until he spoke.

"I rang you this morning. Someone who called herself the housekeeper told me that you'd be out for the day, and when I said it was imperative that I see you, she told me she had booked a table here for you at one o'clock."

"And so you came—why? What—is—urgent?" She lifted her glass and stared into the dark, toffee gold drink with the little sliver of lemon rind.

"Drink your drink, first."

"And get my breath," she said, trying to keep her voice calm. "Because this is quite a moment! You see, I never expected to set eyes on you again!"

"And had no wish to, anyway! I understand. But don't let's pretend. This isn't a friendly meeting. It's a necessity. It's not my heart, it's my head that makes it imperative to speak to you."

"Oh—"

"I wouldn't like to see anyone innocent blindly getting himself involved in a murder if I thought there was the slightest chance of my stopping him."

"And you think I'm doing that?"

"I know you are."

She leaned back in her chair and watched the couple at the next table, an Englishman and a Frenchwoman discussing a play.

"—we'd better choose what we'll eat," she heard Nigel say.

The menu which the waiter had laid before her was large and complicated. Had Rhoda really believed she could have lunched here alone without embarrassment? But then Rhoda perhaps didn't understand the feelings of a girl from the Commonwealth visiting England for the first time.

Vonnie chose *sole veronique*.

"And I seem to remember you like melon. We'll both have that."

The order taken, a white wine chosen, Nigel sat forward, elbows resting on the table and looked deeply at Vonnie.

"Does it occur to you that however angry we may seem with one another, one serious fact remains? By what you've done, you've put yourself in a position of danger. You are a stranger over here, young and inexperienced, and I'd be less than human if I let you continue, like some crazy child, rushing into a nightmare."

"And does it occur to *you*," she countered, "that one week is nearly over and I haven't made a fatal mistake yet? I'll manage. I'll carry out my role and then I'll go back to Canada and nobody will ever know."

"I'm not talking about this masquerade of yours. I'm talking of something far more serious."

"What—" she asked jerkily.

"Isn't it obvious to you, you little idiot?" he cried in low anger. "The police haven't made an arrest yet in connection with Felix Ashlyn's murder. That means they haven't finished their investigations. During the next few days they'll speed up, dig deeper—and find out that you're not who you're pretending to be. Does it occur to you that that makes you very suspect?"

"It has occurred to me," she said crisply, "and if I have to, then I'll tell the truth. The police would surely understand—"

"Something quixotic and beyond the limit of sanity? I doubt it. They'll look on your explanation as a nice bit of self-justifying. And they'll start searching for the real motive."

"And find none," she defended hotly, "since I am not related to the Ashlyns."

"Wheels within wheels within wheels," he said cryptically. "And right in the center, in the hub, the obvious answer. Money!"

"I don't understand. What connection have I with the Ashlyn money?"

"You could be Myra's tool, sent over here because no one would suspect you, as you say, a stranger in the family."

"Sent over here—?" she looked at him in frank puzzlement.

"It's as crazy as anything, I admit that! But nothing is too crazy to be considered by the men who know that the human mind is tunneled with dark twists and turns. Don't you see?"

"No. Go on!"

"I will," he said crisply. "You could have been sent over to England to hasten Joss Ashlyn's death."

"I've—never—heard—" choking, she grabbed her bag and half pushed back her chair.

A hand clamped down on her wrist, making escape difficult.

"I'm not saying what *I* think, or even what the police think. I'm just giving you an idea of the kind of tunnelings the C.I.D. do into motives in a case of this kind. The most seemingly absurd, the most outrageous, must have a hearing. Such an idea as I gave you may never occur to them. But if they've come up against a blank wall in their investigations they're going to widen them. And that'll include you and then everything will be known. Vonnie, tell your uncle the truth before the police force you to! That's what I had to see you for. Tell him. For heaven's sake, the worst he can do is to send you back to Canada!"

"You seem to forget that he's a sick man. He has a bad heart condition."

"And *you* seem to forget that he'll find out, anyway. Honesty from you now will be infinitely better than if the police break the news to him."

Fat, luscious slices of golden melon were set before them with little dishes of ginger and sugar.

Vonnie could smell the cool sweetness of the fruit.

"Why are you bothering?"

"I've told you. I don't want to see you in more trouble than you have to be."

"Thank you." Her tone was cold.

"Don't thank me," he told her without feeling. "It's my wretched conscience that urges me."

"Of course, your conscience!" She spoke with eyes cast down because if she looked at him, she might burst idiotically into tears.

161

"By the way, who suggested that you come here to lunch?" he asked with interest.

"Rhoda."

"Well, it's not the happiest of choices for a woman alone. She should have selected a Regent Street store's restaurant or some place like that."

"She said that as I would be near Soho this morning I ought to try one of its restaurants."

"Rhoda is the housekeeper, isn't she?"

"Yes."

"There seem to be a lot of women in that house!"

She let it pass. The melon looked good and she supposed it tasted good, too. But misery gave the flavor of straw to everything.

"And now," said Nigel. "let's talk of ordinary things and while we do, you can just shut off a part of your mind and let it concern itself with my suggestion that you tell Joss Ashlyn who you are. Then, when we've finished lunch, you can tell me what you've decided."

"I can tell you now. I'll take a risk on the police finding out."

"I could shake you," he said with quiet violence. "Pick up that spoon and get on with your melon. We'll talk about it again later."

"What's the use? Nothing you can say will change my plans. And since there's nothing more between us than—"

"Than my interference. Well?"

"I don't see that we can enjoy lunch together."

"Nevertheless you're going to stay and eat. Just for once, Vonnie, you're going to do as you're told."

"In other words, I'm not only deceitful, and a liar. I'm headstrong—"

"You damned well are!"

"I told you, once before, didn't I, that you liked playing God?"

He gave a little push to his plate, left half his melon and lit a cigarette.

"And what are *you* trying to be? A kind of Lady

162

Bountiful, going around doing good according to your lights?"

"You can mock!"

"I can, can't I?" he agreed icily.

The fish came and with it a sparkling white wine. Vonnie looked at the bottle and had an impulse to seize it and drain it and see what it felt like to be drunk. Perhaps to be drunk on white wine would make you gay, would make nothing matter very much. Perhaps then she would be able to talk and laugh and charm her way back into Nigel's heart. . . .

When the waiter had poured out her glass she seized it and drank. Over the rim she saw Nigel looking at her curiously.

She said, stiffly, "All right! I know you don't drink wine as though it were a glass of milk. I'm not a complete unsophisticate. I happen—to—to want to know what it feels like—" and then the small moment of mounting hysteria went out of her. "Oh Nigel!" she said in a shaken voice and turned her face away.

"Eat your fish."

The calm, matter-of-fact order brought composure back. She turned and picked up her knife and fork.

"It—looks—good—" she said in a small, strained voice.

"It *is* good."

Suddenly Nigel began talking as though they were just two friends, meeting with pleasure. He told her he was back at work and that there was talk of sending him out to India for a while.

She forced herself to be interested.

"You'd like that?"

"Very much. The East has always drawn me. I want to visit it and soak myself in its atmosphere before it gets spoiled by too much Westernization."

"You sound as though you don't approve of progress."

"What is progress? Making airplanes, traveling faster than sound, making H-bombs?"

He was looking away from her as he spoke, his face

grave, preoccupied. She watched him, seeing in this moment another side of him.

"Or isn't progress learning something about the quieter philosophies," he went on. "Knowing how to be happy, how to keep something quiet and still inside oneself so that whatever happens, you're never quite lost? Knowing how to live with yourself—"

"And you think you can do that?" She heard the touch of irritability in her voice.

"Good heavens, no!" he said impatiently. "But I'd give everything I have to acquire it."

"You'll be away in India a long time?"

"I expect so."

And that, she thought, was the end! Now she knew, by the happy note in his voice, that she did not enter, even remotely, into his future scheme of living. It was quite, quite dead, all the love and the promise and the joy that had fused them in that remote world on the shores of the Pacific. . . .

After the fish course, Vonnie could manage no more. They had coffee and conversation dwindled. She was terribly aware of Nigel sitting on the opposite side of the little table, his face grave, his eyes steady and impersonal and the scar livid across his hand.

She refused a liqueur and burned her throat by drinking her coffee almost as soon as it was poured out.

"I think," she said, and made a play of glancing at her wrist watch, "I'll have to go. I'm taking myself to a matinée this afternoon."

It had only just occurred to her to go because she knew that it would be impossible to spend the afternoon at ordinary sightseeing. A theatre would perhaps force her to take her attention from herself.

Nigel was signaling to the waiter for the bill. When he said, "So I haven't been able to change your mind for you?"

"No."

He shrugged.

"Oh well, at least I tried. It's all on your head now. And heaven help you!"

"Perhaps it will," she said quietly, "since my motive wasn't a wrong one."

"You think goodness is rewarded and badness punished, just like that?" he flicked his fingers. "Like some pretty fairy tale? You think you can go ahead with your masquerade and that, if it is found out, everyone will understand and love you for what you did? For God's sake, Vonnie, this is a hard world! It isn't a world of understanding. It has no time for lights and shades of altruism. And it's time you faced it. Grow up, Vonnie, grow up!"

Something flashed through her mind. She said, as though speaking from some far, impersonal philosophy, "It's odd, isn't it? We're told to grow up. To become adult. And yet, in the Bible, we are told that the Kingdom of Heaven lies in being as a little child."

Something flashed and lightened in his eyes.

He said, slowly. "You're a strange girl. Perhaps you're touching more deeply than you realize on a universal truth. I don't know. I'm too grown up, too civilized. That's the hell of it!"

She rose, dragging on her gloves, picked up her handbag.

"Thank you for the lunch, Nigel. I must fly, or I'll be late for the theatre."

"What are you going to see?"

"I don't know," she said and added honestly: "I've only just made up my mind to go."

"If you'll just wait, I'll take you."

"No," she almost shrank away from him. "No, Nigel. Let's say good-bye here."

"Good-bye, then."

They were both standing.

It was the end. There would be no more meetings, no more efforts at understanding. They were a world apart.

His fault? Hers? She turned and walked between the tables and out of the door a waiter held open for her.

The sunlight hurt her eyes. She turned to the left and walked quickly down the street. Nigel made no attempt to follow her.

At the end of Charlotte Street she turned into Shaftesbury Avenue and went into the first theatre that was advertising a matinée.

From a dark seat in the circle she watched the play. She supposed it was amusing because people around her laughed. She sat huddled in her seat and felt alone and defenseless and unloved.

XIV

THE HOT DAYS continued. A few evenings later, Fenella arrived late with Ralph. They had, they said, been to a new restaurant for dinner and Fenella smiled like a replete little cat.

"Lovely food!" she said, "a sort of mixture of French and Spanish."

She sauntered into the drawing room, vital and exotic in a gray dress and a vivid crimson coat. Tiny gold coins glinted in clusters in her ears and her black hair gleamed in the low, late evening sunlight.

"Any developments today?" she asked old Joss.

"None."

Rhoda, in her chair near the window, glanced across at him.

"There *is* one thing. I forgot to tell you. I've been trying to make up my mind whether it's important or not. I found a button, a very charming button made of glass with a tiny bird painted on it. It was lying under the rhododendrons on the side path."

"Does it belong to anyone here?"

Her gaze flicked to Vonnie.

"Apparently not. Fenella hasn't a suit or a dress with buttons like that on it and Myra says it isn't hers—"

She broke off the sentence as though expecting to be interrupted. Vonnie said nothing. She hoped she looked as though it wasn't important.

"You must let Inspector Vachell see it," old Joss said.

"It might," Fenella said eagerly, "have some link with this mysterious woman seen in the garden on the night Uncle Felix was killed."

"On the other hand, it might have no connection at all," Joss put in. "But the least thing, small though it may seem, must be reported."

"Very well," Rhoda was feeling in her small moiré handbag. "Look. Here it is. It's pretty, isn't it?"

Vonnie held her breath. No one, except Rhoda herself and Joss, had seen this suit and an old man would be very unlikely to be so observant as to notice details.

"For anyone who likes fancy buttons, it's charming," Fenella observed lightly. "Personally, I hate them. I loathe fussiness in dress," and then her eyes suddenly widened and narrowed as though she had remembered something. Her gaze moved from the button very slowly and settled on Vonnie. For a moment it was as though she was going to speak. Then she turned deliberately to Ralph and held out her hand.

"I want a cigarette, please."

In the minute's diversion, while Ralph lit cigarettes and Rhoda put the button back in her handbag, Vonnie sought for a reason for Fenella's cool knowing stare. There could be only one. She had seen those buttons on her suit. But she had not worn it before that day when Rhoda saw it and Fenella had not been there. Then sometime or other, she must have snooped in her wardrobe, curious as to her Canadian cousin's clothes. That was it, of course! So Fenella knew and Rhoda knew—and either could be most dangerous if she chose to be her enemy.

Fenella, however, gave nothing away. She sat back relaxed in her chair, accepted a long iced drink, and said a little fretfully that the weather seemed to be changing.

"That's the worst of our climate! We have an unseasonable heat wave and then the winds blow or it drizzles with rain and everyone says: 'Oh, that's how the English girls get their lovely complexions!' Give me hot sunshine —I'll buy my complexion from the beauty counters!"

Everyone laughed. It was one of the few moments of laughter, Vonnie thought, since she had entered the house; a rare light touch, a moment of relaxation to relieve the tension of a murder.

And then the lightness was snapped off sharply as Fenella asked, "Uncle Joss, do you remember painting a portrait of Myra when she was very small?"

"I did, didn't I? I wonder what happened to it?"

"It's probably still in your studio somewhere," Fenella remarked doubtfully, as though she didn't know! As though she and Ralph had not searched for it and found it!

"I must dig it out," he smiled across at Vonnie. "You'd like to see what you looked like as a little girl, wouldn't you? Your hair was much lighter, nearly golden. But then hair often darkens as we grow older. You had the loveliest skin—you still have, of course—and the temper of a little shrew."

"Shall I go and see if I can find the portrait?" Fenella offered, innocently and too eagerly.

"Not now. Leave everything as it is in there. We don't know yet if the police might want another look."

"But they've unsealed the room?" Ralph asked.

"Yes. All the same, there's just a chance that if we go in there we might disturb something that could still be helpful to them."

"Rhoda goes in there," Fenella said. "She could disturb things when she dusts."

"I doubt if she does," Joss said easily, and leaned forward, playing with the knob of the television. Fenella asked, a little boredly. "What's on tonight?"

"A political debate."

"Oh no!" She rose and picked up her glass. "Not for me anyway! Coming, Ralph?"

"I'd like to watch, if your uncle doesn't mind."

"Of course not. And you too, Rhoda?"

"Politics interest me," she said, crossing slender ankles.

"You can have them!" retorted Fenella. "They bore me to death. A lot of men talking about things I'm not the

169

least interested in. Come, Myra, let's go into the garden room."

As well go there as anywhere, Vonnie thought, and followed her, carrying the long half drunk glass of iced orange and soda.

Fenella flung herself down in one of the garden chairs, reached for a yellow cotton cushion on the bench along the wall and tucked it at her back. Vonnie perched on the window seat.

"Cigarette?"

"No thanks."

Fenella smokes a lot, she thought, not for the first time.

"You're a stranger here," she began, "tell me, what do you think of Rhoda?"

"She's very attractive and very efficient."

"Oh, she's all that!" Fenella dismissed the appraisal airily. "Shakespeare had a Dark Lady of the Sonnets. Uncle Joss has *his* dark lady. Rhoda!"

"Why do you say that? Oh, of course," she added, enlightened, "you mean because you think he knew her years ago and—"

"And was in love with her—or rather had an affair with her? I wasn't thinking of that, though, of course, it's true. I was thinking of tonight—the way she brought that button out."

"I don't understand—" Vonnie began.

Fenella's eyes were narrowed behind the little curls of smoke drifting with the draught at right angles across the room.

"She found something that she hoped would identify the woman Greta says she saw that night in the garden."

"Don't you—too—hope that it'll help in—an identification?" For the life of her Vonnie couldn't check the nervous hesitation in her voice.

"Oh yes. But it's the way it was done. As though she had timed the dramatic moment of revelation, as though it was important that she showed us the button when we were all together."

"She—Rhoda, I mean—" Vonnie let out a deep, unsteady breath, "showed me the button earlier."

"She *did?*" Fenella lifted her glass and took a long drink of icy orange. Over the rim, her eyes were leveled at Vonnie.

It was the way she looked at her that finally convinced Vonnie that Fenella knew she had a suit with little painted glass buttons on it. But she must tell her about that suit as though she had no idea Fenella had seen it. Seem honest, as though the whole thing amused her a little.

"I think the reason she showed me," she said as steadily as she could, "is because I had on a suit with identical buttons. She thought I must have lost one."

"And had you?"

"No. Mine were all there."

"That's odd, isn't it? I suppose—" she paused, biting her lips, staring at the dark red rubber covering the floor.

"You suppose—what?"

"I suppose she did—find it where she said, I mean."

"Why should she lie about it?"

Fenella looked at her scornfully.

"For heaven's sake, there could be a whole mass of reasons."

"I'm dull," Vonnie said quietly. "You'd better tell me."

"The most important is that she could have got hold of that button somehow and then *said* she found it in the garden. She might even have 'planted' it there and hoped that someone would see her pick it up."

"But why?"

"To implicate someone else, dear!" Fenella said with exasperated impatience. "Or, if you want it more plainly, to draw suspicion from herself."

"But you don't suspect Rhoda?"

"Yes," Fenella said succinctly.

Vonnie stared at her. Here was someone coming out into the open at last and having the courage—or the audacity—to name his suspect.

"Don't get me wrong," Fenella said smoothly. "I suspect everyone—even you, and Ralph and Uncle Joss himself. Every single one. Because—it must be someone. And, if you want the truth, I'd rather it have been Rhoda than anyone else."

"But that's horrible!"

The beautiful face framed by the silky, raven dark hair did not soften.

"Not so horrible as Uncle Felix dying!" she shuddered.

"It's no use accusing anyone unless you can find a motive, and how could Rhoda possibly have one?"

Even as Vonnie spoke, she knew the possible motive. Money! Rhoda might know that Joss was leaving her well provided for. She heard Fenella explaining it that very way.

"A legacy. A nice fat one, perhaps, to make up for the fact that in his wilder days he never made an honest woman of her! It's obvious."

"And as obvious," Vonnie found herself fiercely protecting a woman she scarcely knew and scarcely liked, "as the fact that it could be anyone else who was named in the will."

"But we don't know what Uncle Joss is doing with his money and I'm ready to guess Rhoda does. I'm pretty certain he talked to her about it when he was ill and thought he was dying."

Vonnie sat back and stared out of the window onto the darkening lawn.

Horrible as it might be, if Fenella was right, then that button might not have slid out of her pocket as she pulled out her hands on the night in the garden. It could have dropped on the floor in her room, and Rhoda could have found it there and picked it up and used it against her. *Used in evidence against her* . . . she who could so easily be exposed as an imposter . . . But Rhoda couldn't know she had been the girl in the garden that night! Doubt tore at her. Suppose Rhoda did know, had seen her, and instead of telling, was waiting for her to admit it? Over a week had passed since Vonnie had come to this house and perhaps Rhoda was getting impatient and the button was a warning. *I know, and if you don't tell, I will!*

Vonnie changed the subject a little too suddenly and with too much emphasis. She crossed to the gramophone.

"Uncle Joss has some nice records."

"Yes, if you like the old classics," Fenella said disinterestedly. "Personally, I don't. Ralph and I go in for modern music. He has a wonderful gramophone upstairs, all wired for stereophonic sound. It doesn't worry Uncle because it's right at the top of the house and he says he scarcely hears it."

"It's good for Uncle to have Ralph here. A man around is company for him," Vonnie said, to draw her out.

Fenella did not answer for a moment. She lay in the long chair, her slender ankles crossed on the foot rest, her fingers drumming lightly on the arm.

Then she laughed.

"Oh, Ralph's good company. I'll grant him that. It's a pity he's not more ingenious."

"Ingenious?"

The dark head rested against the high back of the chair.

"If he were, he'd make more money. He's clever but he hasn't got the knack of starting from scratch. Give him ten thousand pounds and he'd open a business and make it fifty thousand. With no start, he just can't get going."

"It could be that he's not really ambitious."

"Oh he's that, all right," her brilliant eyes lifted and regarded Vonnie. "You've probably guessed that there's quite something between us."

"There is?" Vonnie pretended utter ignorance.

"We would have been married if he had been in a better financial position."

"No love in a cottage for you?"

"No love in a cottage, dear. No kitchen sink and bed-making for Fenella! That's why, after a quarrel, we acted like civilized beings. We talked it out, decided that, though we loved one another, neither of us was prepared to face drudgery and the dullness of too little money. So, we stayed friends. But we both know that if things changed for either of us—for Ralph *or* me—we'd be married tomorrow."

So now she knew what kept them apart! Now she could interpret those strange intense exchanges she had surprised between them, the sensation of a pull and draw of something dynamic. Now she understood Ralph's hints and evasions.

If old Joss had died, maybe everything would have changed for them. Myra had said that her uncle had made a very great deal of money out of painting portraits. And in his will, who benefited most? Fenella? Rhoda? Myra? The estate might be shared. On the other hand, Myra was a comparative stranger. She would probably inherit very little. And the rest would go to the two women in this house. And half of old Joss's money might be considerable to two young people starting married life....

Fenella's eyes went past her. She said, looking out at the garden:

"I'm mercenary and I admit it. If someone else comes along who has money and whom I like, I'll marry him. But if a miracle happens and one of us is left a good fat sum, enough for Ralph to start a business in a big way, then I'll marry him. It's as simple as that."

"He feels that way, too?"

"Oh, Ralph's a realist!" Fenella said.

So much a realist that he could kill for money? Because he wanted Fenella too badly to wait and risk some other man getting her? Ralph, who had been in his top flat that night, must have heard Felix Ashlyn fall and had let him lie there and die? Ralph whose talk of emigrating could be to fend off just such suspicions?

She shivered and said, "It's getting cold. I'm going to fetch a cardigan."

"And I'm going to see if the men have finished watching that dreary political discussion. Since he gave up painting, Uncle Joss has become mad over politics. Before that he couldn't have cared less who was in power so long as they didn't increase his income tax! Selfishness runs in the family, dear. Are *you* selfish?"

"We all are!" Vonnie said vaguely.

"Only some are worse than others," she stretched and rose. "Go and get your coat if you're cold. Ralph and I will probably go up to his flat and play the gramophone. I hope we won't disturb you if you're going to bed early."

"Not in the least," Vonnie said politely. "I read till all hours, anyway."

She stayed a while in her room, sorting nylons to wash, a slip to mend. Fenella had said that Ralph was in love with her. But only a day ago he had sat on the grass and asked Vonnie about Canada. Quite clearly, she heard the echo of his words: "If I go to Canada, I go alone!"

THERE WERE nearly three more weeks to be got through. There was also the threat of police questioning.

Late the following afternoon Vonnie returned from a visit to the London Planetarium.

They were all assembled in the drawing room—old Joss and Rhoda, Fenella and Ralph. As soon as she entered, she knew by their glances that something had happened that concerned her.

Joss told her when she had settled herself, "Inspector Vachell was here an hour or so ago. He wants to have a chat with you, Myra."

It had come! Now for the truth. Nigel had warned her and she had not heeded it. She had taken a chance on the police leaving her alone—she, the stranger to England with nothing to link her with the Ashlyn tragedy. How wrong had she been?

"You don't have to worry," old Joss said kindly. "They only want to ask you a few routine questions."

Such as—'When did you arrive in England? . . . May we see your passport? . . . And the button? May we look through your wardrobe, Miss Ashlyn?'

She felt Rhoda's eyes on her, blank and speculative. Fenella was playing with the pages of a magazine. Ralph, long legs crossed, was staring down at the rug as though the most important thing was the working out of its intricate geometrical pattern.

Rhoda rose, said, "I'd better see about dinner. It's all ready to dish up."

"Well have it, then. The inspector said he'd be calling

early this evening and we don't want an interrupted meal."

Vonnie had a feeling, throughout dinner, that they all all sensed an approaching climax. It was a tension in the air, like the closing of great black wings drawing them in, stifling them. Fenella talked a lot, laughing a little too loudly; Ralph tried to match her gaiety with his own and managed only to be a little facetious. Old Joss was very silent and Rhoda sat, still and calm and watchful at the opposite end of the table.

They were having coffee in the living room when the doorbell rang.

Joss said, "I thought I heard a car. That must be the police."

Rhoda went to the door. They sat there like dummies in a shop window, stiff and listening.

Then Rhoda came back.

"It's someone for you, Myra."

"The police!"

"No, a man. A friend."

A friend? Who, this time? Nigel, or someone else? Someone from Vancouver arrived here and tracing her by that newspaper report of her arrival?

She jumped up so quickly that she nearly lost her balance and pitched over the thick old-fashioned white bearskin rug.

Her heart hammered and her knees went soft. She managed to get to the door, closed it behind her and looked up and saw Nigel. Suddenly, desperately she didn't want to see him. She couldn't control the despairing fury of her voice:

"What have you come for this time? Why can't you leave me alone?"

"I want to talk to you."

"Not again! I can't take it! she cried wearily.

"Get your coat.

"No. Nigel, please—

His hand came out and caught hers. He said, in a low,

gentle voice, "I won't hurt you, Vonnie. Not this time! Please—" he was pleading. "Please come!"

There was a sound outside. They both paused and listened. Nigel's fingers were still closed round her palm. Then men's footsteps tramped across the gravel drive. Someone rang the bell.

Vonnie said weakly, "It's the police. They said they were coming. They want to interview me."

She wrenched herself away from Nigel and turning, clutched the banister for support.

In the living room she heard someone stir. Then the bell rang again.

It was Nigel who crossed the hall and opened the door.

As he did so, Vonnie fled to the little cloakroom to get her coat. Perhaps Inspector Vachell would speak to Uncle Joss first. And while he did, she would go with Nigel, hear why he had come and then pocket her pride and her hurt, and ask him to advise her over her ordeal with the police. She had no one else here in England to whom she could go. Her loneliness, her isolation and her fear were complete.

The cloakroom had no window and was in darkness. She heard Inspector Vachell go into the drawing room. She reached out to lift down her coat from a hanger and as she did so, the cat sprang out with a loud protest at being shut in, and tripped her. She put out her hand to steady herself and clutched at something soft hanging on one of the pegs. Then she gave a sharp cry of pain, snatched her hand away and nearly lost her balance. She pulled herself up and flicking on the light, saw that something had gashed the palm of her hand.

"What's the matter?" Nigel had closed the front door and was by her side.

"There's something here—" She reached for Fenella's furs.

"That cut you? Let me see." Nigel took them from her. "Put your hand under the tap for a moment."

While she held her palm under the cold water, she watched Nigel's fingers probe deeply into the soft pelts of Fenella's stone marten furs.

"I grabbed rather hard," she said, "to stop myself falling."

Nigel said, "Ah!" and pulled something out.

He held it up. It was a little pointed spear of emerald glass.

"This is what tore at your hand. It was deeply embedded—"

"What have you got there?"

They both turned simultaneously.

Inspector Vachell, who had ears and eyes everywhere, was standing in the hall, watching them.

"Miss—Ashlyn—" Nigel hesitated over the name, "came in here to get her coat. She tripped and fell rather heavily against these furs. This piece of glass was caught in them and she has cut her hand. She needs a bandage—"

"Rhoda keeps a first aid box." Uncle Joss towered behind the inspector. "Myra, go and let her see to it."

But Vonnie stayed where she was, numbing her hand with the cold water. She knew that something significant had just happened, like the last piece of a jigsaw puzzle waiting to be put into place. But where *was* the place?

The small chip of emerald glass—stained glass—lay in Nigel's hand.

Fenella's light voice came from the living room.

"What's happening out here?"

Suddenly the hall seemed full of people. Everyone had crowded out. Behind the inspector, Sergeant Matthews looked smug and purposeful and capable of physically overpowering them all.

"Whose are these?" The inspector had taken the furs from Nigel. He held them in one hand, then he took the piece of glass.

"They're mine," said Fenella watching him. "Why?"

"Miss Ashlyn has cut herself," said the inspector gently. "This," he held up the sliver of glass, "was embedded in

179

your fur," he paused. Then in a completely changed voice, cold and authoritative, he shot at her, "How did it get there?"

"I don't know!"

Fenella's eyes were enormous; her hands were smoothing her red silk dress over slender thighs as though she were wiping damp palms.

"But you do, Miss Ashlyn, don't you?"

She stared at the inspector without speaking; an incredulous smile played around her crimson mouth.

"You were here, in this house, on the night your uncle died, weren't you?" The inspector's eyes were no longer gentle and deceptively diffident. They glinted like a hunter after his quarry.

"Of course I wasn't here—I told you—"

"Don't lie, Miss Ashlyn. You were visiting Mr. Winslow. And some time later that evening you traveled with him in his car."

"Certainly I did. We're friends. There's no law against—"

The inspector cut her short.

"We've examined Mr. Winslow's car. On the floor by the passenger seat we found particles of crushed glass, colored glass that must have come from the soles of shoes that trod the studio floor after Mr. Ashlyn was found dead."

Fenella's hand went to her mouth, "In Ralph's car? Then he—oh, oh *no!*"

There was a sound on the stairs. Every head turned— Vonnie saw that Ralph had moved and was on the second step, poised there, taut as an arrow in a bow.

No one spoke for a moment. Then Fenella cried again: "It wasn't you, Ralph, was it? You *couldn't*—"

"Couldn't what, for heaven's sake?" his voice vibrated. "What are you trying to infer?"

The inspector interrupted their small scene.

"Mr. Winslow used the driving seat. There was no glass on the floor on that side. *You* sat in the passenger seat, Miss Ashlyn. The particles of glass were from *your* shoes."

Her eyes darted to Ralph.

"You got in the car on the passenger side, didn't you, Ralph? I remember that night—"

"For God's sake, what are you saying?"

Again the inspector cut in.

"You were in the house on the night your uncle died, Miss Ashlyn, visiting Mr. Winslow. You were anxious to know if any of the brandy had been touched, so you went into the studio and you found your Uncle Felix lying on the floor. Only *you* can tell us if he was already dead. When he was found he was wearing a dressing gown of your Uncle Joss's. That was why, until you bent down and turned him over, you had no idea you had killed the wrong man."

"You have a fantastic imagination, Inspector!" Fenella said with a cold, unshaken defiance.

He was unperturbed. Behind him, his sergeant had closed in quietly.

"Whether from fastidiousness or caution that you might leave your fingerprints somewhere, I don't know," Inspector Vachell continued, "but as you had no gloves with you, you used your furs over your fingers to turn your uncle over to see if he were really dead. *Was* he, Miss Ashlyn? Was he dead? Or did you leave him to die?"

She stood, stiff and straight, staring at him.

He held up the piece of glass. "That, I figure, is how this piece of glass became embedded in your furs."

Ralph stirred on the stairs.

"When I picked you up later that night you knew he was lying there—Fenella, you knew, *and you said nothing!*"

"And you, Mr. Winslow," the inspector turned to him, "denied having been in the house at that time!"

"I was only there for a few minutes. I dashed in and out again. I had to go out and have a drink with a man.

181

Then I returned to pick Fenella up. She was to meet me here—she came along the road as I drove up and said she had just arrived and hadn't been waiting in the house for me. I knew nothing about this! Dear God!—I couldn't have left a man lying there!"

"No, Mr. Winslow, I believe you knew nothing. But lying about your movements hasn't helped our inquiries."

"Lying?"

"Yes. Why didn't you tell us you'd been home that night?"

"But I was there only a few minutes. I've told you."

"And Miss Ashlyn came. She went up to your flat and found no one there. Then, feeling safe in an empty house, she went into the studio."

"It's all fine supposition!" she breathed, with soft, ringing mockery.

"If so, how did this chip of glass get into your fur, Miss Ashlyn?"

He stopped and looked again at Fenella. In the dreadful hushed moment, Vonnie moved quietly to Uncle Joss's side and touched his arm.

"Go and get that hand seen to," he whispered.

She took no notice. She had made a bundle of her handkerchief and clenched it over the wound.

Suddenly Fenella seemed to spring alive.

"But I didn't—I *couldn't* kill anyone! I hate death and horror!" she broke off and looked about her. "Uncle Joss, Ralph—you both believe me—" her voice failed her as in each case their eyes turned from her.

She looked wildly round. The sergeant was too near her for escape. She swung back, her eyes blazing.

"I didn't want to kill anyone! Uncle Felix died as the result of an allergy. You've proved that!"

"Go on, Miss Ashlyn. You didn't want to kill anyone . . . ?"

Behind the fine brow with its dark fringe, Fenella's bright brain was working. Even in defeat, she was defiant.

182

"If I tell you the truth, you'll see that I'm innocent of murder. All right! I *did* put something in the brandy—something that's quite harmless to almost everyone, but would upset Uncle Joss just a little because of his allergy. They were some sleeping tablets I'd once been given and they had the urea derivative Uncle Joss was allergic to. I knew he never let people sit around talking in his studio and that he kept the brandy there for his own use. I crushed them into powder."

"Why did you do it?"

She was silent; her eyes went to Vonnie.

Ralph cried, "Oh, Fenella!"

She swung around on him.

I did it for you as well as myself. For both of us!"

"Why, Miss Ashlyn?"

She took a long breath.

"I wanted Uncle Joss to feel slightly ill—just enough not to want a stranger coming to the house. And she *is* a stranger!" Her eyes were back on Vonnie, narrowed with enmity. "I thought perhaps he'd drink some of the brandy and get ill before Myra left Canada so that he could cable her not to come until he was a little better. I thought I could persuade him to keep her away. Only he didn't touch it for days. I used to go in and shake the bottle so that he wouldn't see the sediment. And then Myra arrived—and you know the rest." She broke off and cried in a burst of bitterness. "Why *should* she come—after all these years, to cash in—"

To cash in! That had been at the root of it. *To cash in. . . .*

Vonnie heard Uncle Joss echo Ralph's words.

"Oh, Fenella!"

The girl turned to him.

"She only came for your money. That's all I wanted to do—just to stop her coming. I didn't mean anyone to die—I didn't—how could I? Death—" She gave a long terrible shudder.

"Only your uncles were twins and they had the same

183

allergy," said the inspector. "Your Uncle Felix had obviously drunk quite a bit from that bottle over the two days he was here. He might have thought that drinks from the bottle in the studio wouldn't have been as noticeable as if he took drinks from the dining room. He must have realized that he was ill after that first drink, but he didn't put it down to the brandy. He wasn't to know that those great bruises on his body were a warning. Why should he? He could have had no idea he had an allergy. It's a very rare one, anyway. The bottle stood on that corner table away from the light so he wouldn't see the sediment. Poison is often a woman's crime, Miss Ashlyn."

Suddenly everything happened at once. The inspector was asking Fenella to go with him to the police station and she kept crying, "But I didn't mean to kill anyone. . . ."

She was still protesting in a high, terrified voice as they led here away down the steps of the house to make her statement at the police station.

Ralph gave Joss one look.

"I'm sorry, sir. I—"

The old man seemed not to hear him. He said in a slow, shocked voice, "She had a key. When I was ill, she asked for it so that she didn't have to keep bothering Rhoda who was nursing me. So she could come and go as she liked, and we would never know!"

He walked alone into the living room and Ralph turned and went back up the stairs.

Vonnie and Nigel were alone in the hall.

He said gently, "Go and get that hand seen to."

"I must talk to Uncle Joss," she protested. "I can't rest till he knows about me—about what I've done."

"If you go in like that you'll bleed all over his carpet," Nigel said matter-of-factly. "Vonnie, get your hand bandaged!"

She gave no sign that she even heard him, "But dare I tell Uncle Joss now? Dare I give him another shock right on top of this one? I've made up my mind that he must know, but—"

Nigel had taken her hand and was tying his own handkerchief round it tightly.

"Don't worry!" he said softly, "I think Fenella's uncle must have passed the first shock days ago when he realized the drug was meant for him!"

She held her injured hand close to her body. Now that the climax had come and passed, Vonnie remembered her own dilemma.

"Why did you come tonight?"

He put up his hands and cupped her face.

"When you told me what you'd done, I was too shaken for sane reasoning. As you said, I played God. I only saw my own point of view. After lunch today, I saw it all differently. I knew suddenly that however mad your scheme was, you'd been sincere. It was wrong of you and foolish and quixotic, but it was kind. Oh Vonnie, you little imposter! And, damn it, I still love you!"

The joy after so much was almost too great to bear. She closed her eyes against the stinging tears and leaned weakly against the wall.

Nigel touched her cheek.

"It's all moonshine, you know, Vonnie, that good intention makes a virtue of fraud. Dangerous moonshine!"

"I know that now," she whispered.

"Lessons are often learned the hard way. Yours was. And now—" his hand reached for hers, "will you let me go in and talk to Mr. Ashlyn? I'll tell him the whole story and I'll do it much better than you would!"

"But it's my responsibility!" she protested.

"It's *ours!*" he contracted. "Everything you do from now on is my responsibility, too, heaven help me! Go, you impulsive, romantic little brat!" He gave her a gentle push. "Get that hand seen to and give me a quarter of an hour."

She was too shaken to argue. She walked down the passage to the kitchen with a feeling that nothing was quite real—that all that had happened this past hour was a dream—part-nightmare, part-heaven. Nigel had said, "I still love you." She pushed open the kitchen door and stared, a little bemused, at Rhoda.

"Your hand," Rhoda's smooth, matter-of-fact voice cut through her dazzled mind. "Come along and let me bandage it for you."

Vonnie said, "Thank you, Rhoda," and sat down weakly in a chair.

"It's a very nasty cut." Rhoda's cool efficient fingers cleaned and bandaged the wound. When she had finished, she said, "I heard it all, you know. And that can't have been very pleasant for you! Let's have a cigarette, shall we?"

Lighting them, her eyes flicked to Vonnie's face and quickly away with a surprising gesture of nervousness.

"I may as well tell you, Myra, and get it over!" she paused. "I thought you were the one who wanted to harm Joss. I didn't know how you could have done it if you had arrived in England when you said you did, but I was determined to find out, to trap you if I could. You didn't drop that button, you know, in the garden! I'm sorry, but I found it in your room. I thought it just possible that you were the girl the German maid next door saw in the garden. After all, you could have come to England earlier than you said. If I could have put my hands on your passport, I'd have done that, as well. I'm sorry."

Vonnie said quietly, "Don't be. *I've* got an explanation, too! But I can't tell you till Uncle Joss knows. I suppose everyone suspected everyone else. That's what happens when something violent happens."

Rhoda lifted her fine dark brows.

"And you suspected me? But you don't harm someone you love!"

"So—it's true?"

"Yes, but you don't have to quote me!" she smiled a little ruefully, "Joss may be an old man now, but he's still mortally afraid of being 'caught' by a woman. I think marriage must be his idea of hell! He can't help it, it's an innate thing in him—part of the curious, passionate desire of the artist for freedom. I understand him."

"If you loved Uncle Joss, weren't you scared that whoever tried to harm him might try again?"

"Of course I was. You mightn't have noticed, but I was like a watchdog. I haunted that house; I watched everyone I could, everywhere possible!"

"But Fenella never meant to kill anyone."

"The fact remains she did, didn't she?" Rhoda said, "and I, for one, have no pity for her. None! She will find life hard in prison and I'm glad. If she had harmed Joss—much as sometimes I get furious and exasperated with him—I think I'd have killed her myself. But it's all over now. Thank God!"

Vonnie heard a step down the hall. She stiffened and listened. Nigel put his head round the kitchen door.

"You're wanted in the living room, Vonnie."

"*Vonnie?*" Rhoda furrowed her brow.

"It's what I have to explain, Rhoda. But later. And thanks for the bandage." Vonnie escaped, running from the kitchen.

Nigel was by her side. Halfway down the hall, she paused, turning to him, asking, "Is Uncle Joss very angry with me?"

"He's much tougher than you think when it comes to emotional shocks. Vonnie, don't shake so! It's all right. Just be yourself—don't pretend anything. Never—never again!"

"Never!" she said brokenly and reached the drawing room door.

Old Joss was standing there. He put out a hand and drew Vonnie inside.

"Rhoda ties a very good bandage, doesn't she?" he said, examining it.

Vonnie felt her heart thud and crash against her ribs. She dragged her eyes to his face.

"Mr. Ashlyn, I'm sorry. I'm so dreadfully sorry—"

187

"It was foolish, wasn't it?"

"Yes."

"And dangerous, as it happens. But you know the saying that to understand all is to forgive all," he smiled. "You've got a fine advocate in this young man of yours! He's pleaded your cause and he showed me how to understand. It's done now! You're here and Myra is probably getting herself engaged. 'Vonnie'—I like that name. It's gentle."

"I don't know what to say, Mr. Ashlyn. I—"

"*I* do," he cut in. "Just quit calling me 'Mr. Ashlyn.' I was Uncle Joss to you. Let's keep it that way."

"Uncle Joss, you've had one shock on top of another!" she cried.

"I have, haven't I. And it hasn't killed me! I told you I'd fooled the doctors. And now, let's get another thing straight. Will you stay on here, Vonnie, just as you planned?"

"I want to—so much! But you can't mean you want me to."

"It's settled."

"Uncle Joss, what will happen to Fenella?"

He said gravely, "I'll do my best to see she has a good defense lawyer. She can't possibly escape a sentence. It's up to us all to help her—and since you've chosen to identify yourself with my family, I'm including you, Vonnie."

"I'll help if I can—"

"She'll need us all," old Joss said. "Perhaps for the first time in her life, Fenella will look to others for help and kindness and forgiveness."

He continued, "Myra must be told."

"Of course. Do you want me to write to her, Uncle Joss?"

He shook his head.

"I'll do it. Then I can tell her what I think of her mad idea and how it went wrong. And perhaps I'll put it more kindly than I would have done before this young man of yours talked to me! I suppose I'm reaping what I've

sown after all—disinterest in the family all these years, *I*
know! Why should Myra give up a chance of marriage
for my sake? Only she should have told me!"

"She was afraid, because you were ill. She wanted her
chance of happiness but she didn't want to disappoint
you."

"She has a very fertile mind!" he said dryly. "It was her
idea, I take it?"

"Yes! But we both worked out the details."

"You're a little devil for punishment, aren't you, Vonnie?" he grinned down at her. "Taking on a burden like
this *and* taking part blame."

"I wanted to see England," she said gently and looked
at Nigel. "*And I wanted to forget you!* As though I could
ever have done so!"

"So, metaphorically speaking, you put on a mask and
took Myra's place," the old man commented. "And fooled
me. And my job is to forgive! Well—"

"Is it well, Uncle Joss?"

"For you and me, yes. Fenella is our problem now."
She asked, "Do you think Ralph will stand by her?"
He said, "He's kind and charming—and weak. My
guess is that he'll run as far as he can away from her!"

To Canada! she thought.

"By the way, I hear you're getting married."

Vonnie's heart lifted on wings and an inner sunshine
blazed about her.

"If Nigel says so!" she spoke on a breath.

Old Joss heard.

"For goodness' sake, girl, haven't *you* got a say? It
takes two people to agree to marriage."

"I know, but love makes it one decision!" she cried
softly and went to Nigel and leaned a little against him.

"It's wonderful, when it's like that, Uncle Joss! As
though never again do you have to stand alone! You
should try it some time."

"Me?" he hooted. "*Me?* At my age?"

189

Footsteps sounded in the hall. Rhoda paused in the doorway.

"Come in," he called. "We're having a very interesting discussion on marriage."

Rhoda looked at each in turn. Then she began to laugh.

"What's so funny?"

"You—" she cried. "You, discussing marriage!"

"It's an idea," said old Joss slowly. "You know what I've just been told? That in marriage, you never have to stand alone again! I've stood alone all my life. Well—almost all of it. And, you know, I think I'm tottering a bit! Rhoda, your arm," he reached out and took her hand.

By the great open window leading to the garden, Nigel looked at Vonnie. No word was spoken. No word was needed. The deepest language of love is in silence. . . .

If you enjoyed this book, you will surely want to read

K-211 50¢

THE PAVILION AT MONKSHOOD by Anne Maybury

What was the secret of THE PAVILION AT MONKSHOOD? Who—or what—lived behind the closed door, watched over by the grinning, silent statue of Pan . . . ? *Monkshood* was doomed, and Jessica with it, unless she could open the evil door and bring a murderer to justice—a murderer who might be the man she loved!

K-191 50¢

THE BRIDES OF BELLENMORE by Anne Maybury

The brides of Bellenmore shared a secret that bound them together unto death. Was there an answer to the riddle of terror that faced a desperate young girl—a stranger in her own family?

K-244 50¢

THE GOTHIC READER edited by Kurt Singer

Haunting stories of Gothic romance and suspense by the finest writers of chilling fiction today—including a long novelette by Dorothy Eden which has never before been published in the United States.

K-175 50¢

MOURA by Virginia Coffman

A chilling Gothic-mystery-romance in the tradition of *Jane Eyre* and *Rebecca*. A young girl journeys to a huge mansion to protect her former charge from a sinister plot that hovers about the gloomy rooms of the great house. "*Moura* is good enough to satisfy all but the most jaded readers of Gothic horror romance." —*San Francisco Examiner*

If your local dealer is unable to supply you with these books, please use the handy order form on the last page.